Dreamspeaker

1978

976

Dreamspeaker

Anne Cameron

HARBOUR PUBLISHING

Harbour Publishing Co. Ltd.
P.O. Box 219
Madeira Park, BC
V0N 2H0
www.harbourpublishing.com

THE CANADA COUNCIL | LE CONSEIL DES ARTS
FOR THE ARTS | DU CANADA
SINCE 1957 | DEPUIS 1957

Cover design by Roger Handling
Page design by Mary White
Sun Mask image on the front cover
by Robert Kwaksistala
Printed and bound in Canada

BRITISH
COLUMBIA
ARTS COUNCIL
Supported by the Province of British Columbia

Harbour Publishing acknowledges financial support from the Government of Canada through the Book Publishing Industry Development Program and the Canada Council for the Arts, and from the Province of British Columbia through the British Columbia Arts Council and the Book Publisher's Tax Credit through the Ministry of Provincial Revenue.

Library and Archives Canada Cataloguing in Publication

Cameron, Anne, 1938–
    Dreamspeaker / Anne Cameron.

ISBN 1-55017-364-2

    1. Indians of North America—British Columbia—Juvenile fiction.
I. Title.

PS8555.A5187D72 2005   jC813'.54   C2004-907464-4

For Alex
Erin
Pierre
Jo
with love, and with thanks.

And with special gratitude to the Nootka people,
especially the people of the village of Ahousat, for
sharing with me their stories, their lives, and their
truths. James Adams, Mary Little, David Frank, Peter
Webster, and John Jacobson have been particularly
loving and supportive, and to them, their children,
their grandchildren, and the children of Ahousat, this
story, and much love.

1

A LONG SEGMENTED SNAKE OF TRAFFIC moved toward the city, the rush-hour fumes already tainting the face of a morning sun. A blue Pontiac segment, a red Toyota, an orange Datsun, piece by piece, section by section, the serpent twined toward the city and the tall concrete buildings with view windows looking out on other view windows across the canyon that was the street. And leaving the city, moving down the other half of the freeway past the segmented serpent, one or two at a time, a few suburbs-bound cars, one of them a conservative dark sedan with the door decal of the provincial government.

The boy Peter sat pressed tightly against the back of the front seat, his eyes only half focusing on the serpent sliding past on the other half of the freeway. On either side of him, the people: the driver, big, heavy, with cold grey eyes and hands built for grabbing and holding. Hands with fine, light-coloured hairs growing down the backs, down his fingers to the first joint, and his fingernails clipped short, like little shovels at the end of his long, thick fingers. And the woman, not big, not small, not young, not old, her dark hair brushed away from her face, here and there some grey hairs showing,

I could move fast, grab the handle with my left hand, shove it down and at the same time shove her with my right hand and she'd fly off the seat and out the door and maybe get run over by

the car behind us . . . but that would leave him . . . the big hand would just reach out and grab. No chance of shoving him out the door . . . He could feel the driver's eyes flick sideways, knew the grey ice eyes were registering his every breath. *Nothing to watch here, asshole, just me, sitting here as good as gold, watching the snake coming toward us . . . Just Peter, out for a morning ride, that's all . . .* He knew his face showed nothing. His hands were under control and wouldn't betray him.

The woman smiled down at the little boy. Light brown hair, almost blond, his skin so pale that the fine blue veins showed at the temples. A good face, undeniably Anglo-Saxon, the child all white middle-class parents hope will be theirs. Strong, even teeth, shoulders already widening, chest full and promising an adult strength and endurance.

She opened her purse, took out a package of Doublemint gum, pulled one stick partway out of the package and offered it to Peter. His green eyes took in the stick of gum, flicked to her face, then back to the gum. One hand reached out, took the gum; his lips moved to whisper "Thank you," and he stared at the gum. She held the package toward the driver, who reached over with one hand, took a stick, nodded his thanks, and, one-handed, unwrapped the gum and put it in his mouth. His jaws moved strongly as he looked down at the boy, who was still staring at the stick of gum.

Peter began to unwrap his gum, pulling the silver foil-wrapped stick from within the green envelope. He put the green paper carefully on his lap, unwrapped the silver paper and laid it beside the green. Precisely, slowly, he folded the stick of gum in half, then in half again, and then he lifted the gum to his lips, opened his mouth, slid the gum inside and began to chew, almost mechanically, his thin throat swallowing the minty saliva.

His hands, of their own accord, carefully folded the silver foil as if the stick of gum were still inside, then just as carefully slid the silver foil back into the green envelope. Precisely, betraying his nervousness, the fingers folded the paper in two, then again, until finally he had a small squarish ball of paper, which he dropped carefully into the ashtray.

Then he sat back, pressed against the back of the front seat, his eyes staring out the window, his jaws moving rhythmically, almost daintily, his eyes glazing over with the curiously blank stare he wore so often. Eyes unfocused, as if blotting out something he didn't want to see, couldn't be bothered to watch.

The car turned off the freeway, speeding down the exit ramp, turning along the secondary highway.

Anna watched Peter hiding behind his own eyes, remembered the first time she had seen him. Four years old then, his hair hanging shaggy and uncombed past his shoulders, his face thin and smudged with several days' dirt and tears, his clothes smelly and unwashed, too small for him, his overalls held up with pins where the snaps were gone on the shoulder straps. He was barefoot, and when they stripped him down to give him a bath they found a disgustingly filthy diaper ripped from what had once been an old crib sheet. His scrawny buttocks had been covered with diaper rash, deep-pitted pustules amid hot red chafed skin, and his penis swollen with ammonia burns, the head of the penis raw, the shaft pimpled and oozing. When they sat him in a bathtub he wept with pain.

His feet had been thick with callus, his legs flaky with dry skin she thought was eczema. The doctor said no, it was poor diet, dirt and probably dehydration as well. They soaked him in the tub for five or ten minutes, then scrubbed him with strong green soap, ignoring his weeping, scrubbing the pustules even though they bled, and then they washed his hair to be rid of the lice they knew were crawling on his scalp.

When the rinse water cascaded over his face, Peter quit sobbing and looked amazed, even tried to grin.

An hour later, dressed in new clothes, his backside liberally smeared with an antibiotic cream, his hair hanging over his forehead and fluffing out from his face, he sat on a chair in her office and stuffed himself with a McDonald's hamburger, vanilla milkshake and a cookie.

Very little was known about Peter prior to that day. A birth certificate had been found in the mess that was the basement suite in which he had been living. There was no sign of an immunization record, so they had started him on all the shots immediately. His father had apparently abandoned the family at least a year earlier; the mother was vague as to when he had left and where he had gone. Shaking in withdrawal, she had managed to say The bastard took off, what more do you want to know, chrissakes, I'm sick.

Later, when she was over the withdrawal period and receiving medication in the women's section of the prison, she had told them more. At the time it was a new and shocking story to Anna, fresh out of university and new to the job, but in the years since she had heard this story or versions of it so often she no longer really listened.

A drab, fundamentalist childhood, poor school record, and, at fifteen, a runaway. Several casual liaisons with men whose names she didn't remember, two somewhat longer relationships, then, at nineteen, she moved in with the man she said was Peter's father. Alcohol and sex, then drugs and sex, and then both of them were addicted and she was working the streets, trying to feed both their habits while he worked the apartments and houses left vacant when the owners or renters went off to work. Between what he stole and she hooked, they had managed to get from fix to fix.

And then he left. She didn't know why, she didn't know where, and she didn't care.

Peter was alone in the apartment most of the time. She would leave the television going, sometimes remember to leave sandwiches and an open can of soup and a spoon, but often she didn't remember and he went hungry. Her life was a constant search for men, money and heroin. Men and money important only in that they were her access to heroin. Peter didn't count except that by having him she was eligible for welfare; because of him she was assured of some money, however little.

The government vehicle moved down the secondary highway, the traffic lessening, the city giving way to fields and brush. Peter sat, hands folded loosely in his lap, eyes still unfocused, putting in time until they got where they were going. She patted his knee gently, and a brief smile flicked across his face. The driver looked at her expressionlessly and she wondered if he knew anything of what she was feeling.

Peter had been placed temporarily with a foster family and in the few weeks with them he had gained weight, developed some colour in his cheeks and even begun to learn how to play with other children. It was a temporary placement, however, and after he had been officially apprehended for his own protection and placed in wardship, a more permanent arrangement was found for him with another family. A few months later the foster mother became ill and the children placed with her had to be transferred to other homes. Peter didn't fit in as well in his third foster home and it was necessary to place him in a home with fewer children, a home where the foster mother could spend more time with him, particularly trying to toilet train him.

By the time Peter was six he had been in nine foster homes, his toilet training was incomplete, he regularly wet the bed at night and he was subject to sudden, unexplained temper tantrums.

His mother had never visited him in the years since his apprehension and was presently serving a three-year sentence for prostitution and trafficking in narcotics.

The car slowed, turned to the left and rolled up to the high gates that opened to let the car through, then closed behind it again. The car moved up the driveway toward the cluster of buildings and pulled to a halt in front of the administration office.

Peter waited until the woman had opened her door and got out of the car. She stood by the still-open door, waiting. The driver got out, closed his door, then stood beside it looking with satisfaction around the facility. After a moment, Peter slid across the seat and climbed out of the car. For one brief moment he tensed to run, then he relaxed and turned, instead, to the stairs leading up to the aluminum and glass door. *No good running, you wouldn't get ten steps and that big bugger would have you . . .*

The woman put her hand on his shoulder, gently, and walked with him up the front steps and through the door to the long hallway. The driver came behind them, effectively blocking any chance of escape.

The man sitting behind the desk was middle-aged and the smile on his face was reflected in his eyes. The woman sat down and handed the man the thick file she had been carrying. The driver sat down near the door and waited for Peter to try to run away. Peter sat down in a chair next to the woman and waited.

The man behind the desk talked briefly to the woman. What they were saying didn't interest the boy and he let his eyes unfocus, hiding inside himself, his hands idle on his lap again, his face appearing empty. After some minutes the man looked quickly through the file and for a moment Peter's eyes registered the movement of paper, but that, too, had no interest for him and he retreated again to that place where nobody could bother him.

Sometimes he sat like that from one meal to another, and if anyone touched him or spoke to him, he would focus his eyes and come back from where he had been, but when they asked him what he'd been thinking, he couldn't answer. One of the mothers had told him it wasn't possible for a person to think about Nothing, that the brain was working all the time; even when you were asleep you had to be thinking about Something. He supposed this was just another of the ways he was different. Entire days of his life were spent not thinking about anything at all. Sometimes sitting, sometimes standing, all he had to do was unfocus his eyes and time passed by without touching him.

"Come along, Peter." The man came from behind his desk and touched Peter on the shoulder. The boy stood automatically. The driver got up off his chair and cursed softly when he saw the chewing gum stuck to his pants. Peter pretended he didn't know where the gum had come from and followed the man from the office to the hallway. The woman came over to him then and half knelt, her face inches from his, her eyes demanding that he listen.

"I want you to write me little notes, like you used to. Will you do that for me?"

He nodded because it was what she wanted him to do and

he always tried to please her. She was one of the few constants in a changing world. Sooner or later, whatever else happened, he would see her, even if only for a few minutes, and she would talk to him just as if he was anybody else and not himself at all.

She pulled him close and gave him a strong cuddle, not one of those squeezey things some people give when they don't really want to touch you but feel they ought to. "You mustn't worry about things, Peter, everything is going to be fine." She smiled and he wanted to smile back, but couldn't. "We'll keep in touch and in a little while I'll come down and we'll spend an afternoon together, okay?"

Her eyes were sad and he wished he could tell her not to worry. He wished he could touch her, just once, softly, but he couldn't. It wasn't always allowed, and it might be all right for adults to touch a kid, but kids couldn't do things like that to adults unless they knew it was wanted. So his arms hung at his sides and the woman stood up quickly and headed for the doors. She turned with her hand on the door, smiled at him and waved, and he made his arm come halfway up and made his fingers wiggle good-bye, but he still couldn't make his face smile.

At the cottage he was introduced to another man, John, a young man with a big grin, a white tee shirt, blue jeans, white socks and white leather running shoes with three blue stripes on the side. Black hair and almost black eyes, the whiskers on his face shaved off, but you could see the pattern of the beard under his skin. His beard was almost blue, like the tail of a rooster Peter had seen in the zoo.

"Hi, Peter," John said easily, "I'm John and I'm your counsellor. That's sort of like saying I'm the boss, I guess, but I'm not, really." Peter nodded. There wasn't anything to say and there wasn't anything else he could think of doing, so he waited. John talked for a while with the man from the office, and then the man left, probably to go back and sit behind his desk, and John led Peter to the room that was to be his.

A neutral room, white ceiling, cream-coloured walls, the floor covered with dark brown heavy-duty linoleum tile. A single bed, a dresser and a closet. The drapes and counterpane, patterned with hockey players chasing pucks at random, were meant to add a more comfortable, home-like touch, but, Peter noticed, there wasn't even a hint of a goal or a goaltender. He stared at the drapes. He would have liked to have shared the joke with John, but he wasn't sure John would understand. You had to be careful what you said or people would think you were odd. He'd learned that word from one of the mothers—he couldn't remember which mother. A good short word that said it all: odd.

They left his shopping bag of things on his bed and John laid his arm across Peter's shoulders, which is just another way of leading you around, but at least better than holding your hand as if you were a baby. Peter didn't really want to leave his shopping bag behind; what if someone went in the room and took something? He had an old ball glove in there and some comic books and an empty tobacco can. Well, empty of tobacco, but the can was full of bits and pieces of crayon, stubs of pencil and even a small green sharpener. What if someone went in and stole it? If he said that, he knew John would try to reassure him, like the guy at summer camp who stared with round blue eyes and said Oh, we don't steal from each other here, Peter, we're a family. Someone in the family had taken his bullwhip made from kelp, and his collection of shells, and even his spare running shoes and they had never found any of it, even though the runners had his name marked on them with laundry ink. Peter was pretty sure it was the kid with the blond hair hanging to his shoulders, the one with thick glasses with heavy black frames, but he couldn't prove anything.

The man at the supply room gave Peter two pair of grey denim pants, three denim shirts, also grey, and three sets of underwear—jockey shorts and singlet—mercifully not grey but plain white cotton. Six pair of black socks, a pair of ugly black shoes without laces. Not loafers, they were called romeos, and Peter knew they were worn by fishermen and tugboat workers. Black runners for sports and white gym shorts, a white tee shirt and a black bathing suit. Two pyjamas, light blue, a black denim jacket and a grey sweater. In return for which he took all of Peter's clothes and put them in a box, closed the box, wrote Peter's name and a number on it, then stored the box in a cupboard full of other boxes with other names. The two men waited while Peter got dressed in facility clothes, then they went back to his room, he and John, and John waited while Peter put his clothes away in the dresser and closet.

The boy took a long time putting away his clothes. Jeans Just So, the side seams carefully together, the jeans hung over a hanger as if they were dress pants fresh back from the cleaners. The shirts folded Just So and put in a drawer. The sweater in the same drawer as the shirts. Pyjamas in another drawer. Underwear and socks in the top drawer. Jacket hung in the closet, Just So. When everything was put away the boy gravely checked to be sure that things were, in fact, Just So, then he turned and faced the door, waiting. John was struck by the curiously machine-like attitude of the boy, a robot waiting for a button to be pushed so the printed circuits could mesh and move the arms and legs.

The doctor checked the boy thoroughly: heart, lungs, eyes, ears. He palpitated the boy's abdomen and thumped his back, tested his elbows and knees for reflexes, looked down his throat, even put on a rubber glove, lubricated the middle finger and explored the boy's anus. Through it all the boy gave every impression of being somewhere else, his eyes unfocused, his face carefully blank. The doctor took blood from the boy's inner elbow, more blood from the tip of his finger, then handed the boy a small bottle and pointed wordlessly to a doorway. Peter took the bottle and moved carefully across the room, opened the door and went into the bathroom.

Checking over the medical report, the doctor noted out loud that all these tests had been done a number of times before, the latest less than a week earlier when the boy had been apprehended by the police.

The boy came from the washroom with the small bottle half full of urine. Carefully he placed the bottle on the desk, then he stood, waiting patiently, eyes again unfocused.

THE DINING ROOM WAS ALREADY CROWDED WITH BOYS when Peter and John arrived. John explained the routine, but Peter already knew what to do, it was the same as at summer camp. He got a tray and stood in line, speaking to nobody, ignoring the sly glances, the whispers. He took a knife, fork and spoon from the segmented metal utensil container and laid them on his tray. A bowl of soup, then move a few steps and wait until the man in the white pants, white shirt, white apron and funny little white box-cap finished pouring gravy on the potatoes. Take the plate, put it on the tray, move to the next place, get a small plate with a breadbun and a pat of butter. Move to the next place, take a dessert and a large glass of milk, then move to where the messhall supervisor stood and wait until he pointed to a seat at a table.

John leaned against the wall of the dining room, watching. Peter placed the heavy tray on the table, then stepped over the bench and sat down slowly, ignoring the other boys. Carefully he picked up his paper napkin, arranged it Just So on his lap, one corner carefully tucked under the waistband of his jeans. The milk glass in the upper right-hand corner where there was no chance of it getting spilled. Move the plate of dinner to the upper left-hand corner of the tray, the bowl of soup to the front of the tray. The knife and spoon on the right, the fork on the left. Butter the bread carefully. Everything Just So. And only when it was Just So, only then and no sooner, Peter began the serious business of eating his lunch, holding the spoon properly, spooning away from him, as was polite, one hand, his left hand, resting on his lap, politely, his head bent, spooning the soup carefully and paying no attention to anybody else.

A big boy, thirteen or fourteen years old at least, leaned across the table, grinning. Saying nothing, grinning tauntingly. He picked up the salt shaker and held it teasingly over Peter's soup. Peter ignored the boy, ignored the salt shaker, continued to eat. The big boy, aware that everyone was watching him, slowly tipped the salt shaker and several small streams of salt fell from the holes in the lid, fell into Peter's soup. Peter sat back quietly, and when the salt shaker was finally empty he very carefully moved his half-full bowl of soup to the upper left-hand corner of his tray and brought his plate of food to the place in front of him where the soup had been. He took a sip of milk, carefully wiped his mouth with his napkin, then, fork in left hand, knife in right hand, he meticulously cut a slice of meatloaf and lifted it to his mouth, chewing slowly, counting to himself.

Chew each bite one hundred times and you'll never get a belly-ache. Some people said twenty times, some said thirty times, and one mother told him he had the one hundred times mixed up with brushing your hair before you went to bed at night, but he was sure that was what the other mother had told him, chew each bite one hundred times and you'll never get a belly-ache.

The bigger boy watched Peter, his grin disappearing, his blue eyes narrowing, a faint pink growing on his cheeks. He wasn't used to having new fish ignore him, especially little new fish who fritzed and frutzed with their trays before starting to eat. He reached for a second salt shaker and again very deliberately tipped it, pouring salt on Peter's lunch.

The messhall supervisor moved quickly toward the table, but was intercepted by John. The boys at the surrounding tables were craning their necks, half-standing to watch. Peter was unaware of all that; he was chewing carefully, watching the big boy pouring salt on his dinner. Peter looked down at his plate, moving his knife and fork with dainty precision, and cut another piece of meatloaf. The bigger boy's eyes watched every move, followed the fork and its tidy burden of meatloaf and salt from the plate to Peter's mouth. Peter stared back at the boy for a moment, then carefully focused his gaze on the piece of meat, knowing the older boy's gaze was riveted there also.

Then he dropped both fork and meat. The older boy involuntarily flicked his eyes downward, watching the fork fall, and in that moment Peter's left hand shot forward, grabbed the soup bowl and threw it in his face. As the boy yelled and clawed at his eyes, Peter was across the table, his face strangely devoid of emotion, the sugar dispenser in his hand, hitting, hitting, hitting, his eyes slightly narrowed, hitting, knocking the bigger boy off the bench and pounding his head on the floor, pounding and hitting. It was what you had to do or they'd never leave you alone, you had to show them you could stand up for yourself, teach them a bloody good lesson and they'll leave you alone. One of the fathers had told him that, and it always worked. One of the big brothers had shown him the fork trick, only the big brother had used a cigarette and a paper penny match and had said you had to know before you started where you were going to hit. Don't try to punch him in the nose, he had said, you'll only make his nose bleed. Aim for the back of his head and punch right through his nose to get there and you'll drop him every time . . .

John grabbed Peter and lifted him off the already bleeding older boy. As Peter's feet touched the floor he whirled, ready to meet a new threat. When he saw John his arms went limp and he stood quietly, waiting, only his quick breathing betraying any emotion, his eyes unfocused again.

"It's okay, Peter," John said calmly. "He started it. Okay, Ted," he said to the bigger boy. "Get yourself down to the infirmary and get fixed up, then report to Mister Jensen. You others clean up this mess. Maybe next time you'll remember you spent your lunch hour cleaning up and you'll do something to stop it before it goes this far."

"What about my lunch?" Ted snarled, wiping blood from his top lip.

"You couldn't have been very hungry or you'd have been eating instead of instigating. Move!" And in that last word John brought to bear all the authority and power of a counsellor, and

Ted moved away quickly, angry, shamed, knowing he wouldn't do anything about it, knowing the new fish had only been doing what had to be done.

"Go get your lunch, Peter," John said quietly, and Peter moved, obedient, and went to get a new tray.

Then he sat down in the same place at the same table, eating his lunch with unemotional precision, sitting in some kind of lonely dignity while the other boys cleaned up the mess from the fight. He knew they were watching him, but he also knew nobody else would bother him. For a while. They would wait, try to see if his defiance of Ted's bullying was real or something brought on by the tension of a new place, a new situation. He wasn't worried. He'd been through all this before. He knew you made your stand and laid out your ground and then you stuck to it and stuck up for yourself and made them learn to just leave you alone.

THE LOCKER ROOM RESOUNDED WITH NOISE. The boys hurried out of their clothes, cavorting in undershorts, throwing shirts, wrestling for possession of towels, chasing each other around the room, leaping over benches, struggling against the lockers, laughing and shouting.

Peter took off his shoes and socks, tucked the socks inside the shoes and placed the shoes carefully in his assigned locker. He took off his jeans, folding them carefully, seams in line, and placed them on the shelf in the locker, then hung his shirt neatly on a hook. John watched carefully from his position near the far door. The undershirt folded on top of the jeans, just so, the undershorts placed on top of the undershirt. Peter stepped into his bathing trunks, pulling the waist-string tight, tying it carefully.

He closed the locker door, snapping the combination lock shut and repeating to himself for the umpteenth time *six-left-four-right-all-the-way-around-to-five-to-open*. He went to stand by the doorway, watching the other boys wrestling and shouting, cramming their things into lockers, some of them not even bothering to lock their things away safely. When the Pool Warden came to the door and blew his whistle, the boys pushed past Peter to the high-ceilinged pool room and raced for the edge to dive into the water.

Peter walked carefully, obeying the No Running On Pool Deck sign, watching carefully so as not to slip on the wet polished tile. He moved to the diving board, climbed the steps, moved along the board and waited a moment for a group of splashing jokers to swim to one side of the pool, then dove neatly from the board and began to swim back and forth, back and forth, moving in the easy rhythm the instructor at camp had shown them, his head barely moving, his legs kicking strongly from the hip, back and forth from end to end, swimming, as he had been told to do.

Swimming until he was white-faced and breathing jerkily.

"Peter!" John called suddenly, and the boy moved obediently to the side of the pool. John reached down, grasped Peter's arm and pulled him from the water to sit at the edge of the pool, chest heaving, trembling with fatigue, eyes unfocused, face closed.

MOONLIGHT PALE THROUGH THE BEDROOM WINDOW, the carefully neutral anonymity of the room made even more so by the cool, silvery rays. The boy lay curled on his side, his face younger than his eleven years, relaxed and unguarded in sleep.

The door to the room opened briefly and the night-duty

attendant looked in, checked the boy briefly, then left again, closing the door with a slight click.

Peter's eyes opened. He wasn't sure what had wakened him. He lay quietly, hoping to go back to sleep right away. He looked at his hand, decided his fingers looked like petals curling from the centre of a flower. The window was partially open, the breeze coming through the heavy screen making the curtains seem to move, the hockey players endlessly chasing the puck, playing hockey with neither goal nor goalie. *Break away! he heads toward the crease, he winds up, he shoots—he can't score, there's no goal!*

A lightning bug. Only a lightning bug. Peter knew about lightning bugs, had read about them. They were small, some people called them fireflies, and they had them Back East. But how would a firefly or a lightning bug get through the wire mesh? Designed to keep boys in, it would certainly keep shiny bugs out.

Little dots, dancing, bobbing, and a sound like a cricket chirping or a grasshopper rubbing his legs together, or fingernails on a blackboard. Increasingly unpleasant, increasingly insistent, and the bright dots becoming a myriad, forming into a cone, inverting, changing shape, pulsating . . . it was them again. . . and in the corners of the room the shadows gathering, gaining strength from each other, gathering and beginning to move from the corners.

Peter sat up in bed, staring, fright growing in his stomach. Every time the lights and the chirping started, something bad happened. Every time. He pressed against the headboard of the bed watching

ant-small Peter in the middle of the room, surrounded by gigantic forms stretching to the ceiling. A woman, face gaunt, eyes shadowed, screaming from an enormous mouth, her voice shrill and hysterical, screaming Why do you do things like this? . . . Can't you see what you're doing to me? . . . You know I'm not feeling well . . . and a huge man, his face twisted with rage, grabbing ant-Peter by the shoulder, shaking him, roaring Nothing but trouble since the day you were born, Christ, boy, but you're stupid. Policemen with big hands for grabbing and the woman with a file in her hands, mothers tsk-tsking and fathers shaking their heads, exchanging pitying glances with all the big brothers

and something coming from beneath the bed, something long and snake-like, leaving a wet trail on the floor, raising its horned heads, searching, looking both in front and behind, seeing where it was coming from and where it was going, looking hungrily

IN THE MORNING, OF COURSE, THE BED WAS WET, the telltale stain on the bottom sheet betraying Peter wordlessly, the wet pyjama bottoms further proof of his shame.

"Don't worry," John said easily, "we'll get fresh bedding and pyjamas and nobody but us will know about it. Tonight you'll have a rubber sheet. Now come on, breakfast is waiting."

2

LIFE IN THE FACILITY MOVED FROM DAY TO DAY, week to week. New boys arrived and a few boys left, two of the bigger boys ran away and spent several fun-filled days in town before being brought back by the police. They said they had got some girls to go with them to a place they knew, and their whispered stories of what had happened then made the other big boys grin and the smaller boys try hard not to appear puzzled. One boy cut his hand open in carpentry class and the doctor had to stitch him together again, and the psychiatrist came out to the facility to test some of the newer boys.

Peter was one of the boys to be tested. He had walked down the hallway with John, not knowing where he was going or why, and not caring. As soon as he saw the psychiatrist, though, he knew what was going to happen: it had all been done before. So he sat down in the indicated chair, took a couple of deep breaths, and went away for a while. John watched it happen. One moment the boy was his usual poker-faced self, green eyes betraying nothing, the next moment the green eyes were unfocused, blank, the face looked like that of a corpse, and the boy was staring past the desk, past the psychiatrist, past all reality.

Peter stayed like that for fifteen minutes while the psychiatrist tried to find a way through the curtain the boy had pulled.

"Come on, Peter," John finally said quietly, touching the boy's shoulder. Peter blinked, climbed off the chair and moved toward the door.

THE RAKE MOVED OUT CAREFULLY, touched the ground, rustling the fallen arbutus leaves. Peter drew it toward him slowly, then lifted it and moved it away from him carefully. The teeth of the rake left little marks on the soft ground, marks like rivers or roads, moving from one edge of the neat plot to the other, from under the neatly trimmed shrubs and red-peeling arbutus trunks to the edge of the sidewalk. Soon the crocus and snowdrops, daffodils and tulips would poke up out of the dirt and it was very important to get all the little sticks and bits of grass and rock off the soft earth, very important to have this plot of dirt Just So because when the flowers came up you wouldn't be able to just go raking around, you might hurt them, maybe even break off a flower and kill it.

A sudden crash of window glass and Peter froze. He could feel eyes burning into his back, feel fingers pointing at him.

"New kid's fault."

"Yeah, he done it, crazy Pete done it," and a crowcaw chorus of Yeah Yeah Yeah.

He turned stiffly, facing his tormentors, trying hard not to slump, putting his face Just So, refusing to react to anything. John was watching him curiously, waiting for him to say something. Peter wanted to say I didn't do it, but he couldn't speak. He waited. The laughing and giggling continued and then John was talking, still staring at Peter and Peter made his ears listen to what was being said.

"Bullshit." John's voice was soft. "He was raking. It was Rocky and Fred did it."

The two boys began to protest, faces innocent.

"Oh, come off it," John said impatiently. "I'm not blind, I saw it all," and they fell silent, their faces betraying them. "Okay, over to the office, I'm sure they've got all the glass and putty you need to fix it up. And say good-bye to dessert for a week to pay for it." They headed for the office, each one angry with the other for talking him into it.

"Peter." John moved closer, and Peter turned to begin raking again. John stared down at the boy's back. "Peter, you didn't even try to defend yourself . . ." and Peter wanted to turn around, look in John's eyes and explain why he had said nothing, but he couldn't make himself turn around. Finally John got tired of staring down at Peter's back, and he moved away, hurt and puzzled.

The rake moved out carefully, touched the ground softly. Peter drew it toward him slowly, then lifted it and moved it away again, carefully reaching under one of the shrubs.

There was a face hidden in the leaves, the eye clearly defined in the curve of a twig. A face. Staring at him. The firefly-lightning bug lights began to dance around his head and the cricket-grasshopper twittering began ringing in his ears and skull as the fog-like body began to come out of the camouflage of careful tidy lines. Pulling itself together, coming toward him, sliding up the rake handle, slithering along his arms . . .

His feet began to try to back away from it, but his legs didn't want to move. He could hear small sounds coming from his throat, could feel his arms jerking in protest, and part of his mind was aware of John, staring at him, horrified. From the head, the closest head, a dark fog moving toward him, wrapping around his throat and face, smothering him, his hands trying to pry the stinking slime . . .

"Get the doctor," John yelled, and the boys all ran for the office, terrified.

Peter was sprawled on the sidewalk, his fingers clawing his throat, his entire body convulsing. Spittle formed at the corners of his tightly clenched mouth and dribbled over his cheeks and chin. John knelt beside him, whipping his belt from his pants, feeling with his thumbs for the pressure points under the jaws, forcing the jaws open and pushing the belt between Peter's teeth. He rolled the boy on his left side, not trying to stop the threshing limbs, merely trying to make the boy as comfortable as possible while the seizure lasted.

When he realized the seizure wasn't passing, that the boy was not having a standard convulsion but was choking to death, John grabbed Peter in his arms and ran for the infirmary.

The nurse handed the doctor a shining curved instrument, and then a gurgling sound, like a plugged sink being cleared. An airway inserted, nostrils cleared and something that looked like swimmers' nose plugs aiming oxygen up the nose, a long needle directly through the chest, the doctor talking softly all the time, soothing the boy with the sound of his voice, and then a long gasping sigh and Peter relaxed, exhausted, his face pale, his fair hair damp with sweat, eyes dark rimmed, lips swollen and bruised.

PETER OPENED HIS EYES, looked into the soft smile of the evening nurse. She was wiping his forehead, smoothing his hair, and there was a perfume clinging to her skin that brought dim memories of one of the mothers—he couldn't remember which one. One day he wanted to see all those mothers again, to tell them what he hadn't been able to tell them before, what he couldn't tell John, or the evening nurse, or even Anna.

The nurse tucked the blankets around his shoulders, patted his cheek softly, smiled at him again and left, and he closed his eyes, wanting to go back to sleep. His eyes wouldn't stay closed, the lids jerked open again. He could see the furniture: one or two other beds, some sidetables, a chair with his clothes folded neatly on the seat. He could hear a radio playing softly somewhere down the hallway.

He remembered the thing coming out of the leaves and leaping for his throat. Remembered the stale, swampy odour, the jellymass clogging his nostrils and both John and the doctor saying It's all right, son, it's all right

but it wasn't

already it was in the hospital. It had escaped the machine that had sucked it off him, it was in the walls, slithering from room to room, following the electric wires, going from place to place. Looking. Looking for him.

THE FACILITY WAS HALF LIT FOR THE NIGHT, the rooms in darkness, the corridors still bright. Night dew on the bushes and grass, a faint breeze playing tag with the leaves, and high above, long grey clouds scudding across the face of the moon.

Peter dodged easily from shrub to shrub, keeping low, moving only in short bursts, threading his way surely toward the high fence around the perimeter of the facility. Just like hide and seek at night with the foster brothers and the kids down the road, and the rules the same: stay off the gravel, don't run on your heels, flatten yourself if you hear Anything . . .

He waited by the big tree and looked back at the facility. Nobody was watching from any of the windows, nobody was out on the lawn, but he knew it wouldn't be long before the nurse went back into the room and saw the empty bed and the missing clothes.

He ran down the slightly sloping lawn, heading for the fence, and the firefly-lightning bugs began to form at the outer periphery of his vision. What sounded like the faint song of frogs, wasn't. Peter knew what it was, and he was afraid to look behind in case he saw the thing coming across the dew-damp grass, both heads aiming for him.

The wire mesh bit into his fingers, the heavy facility-issue shoes didn't fit the diamond-shaped openings in the crusader fence, his shoulders ached with pulling himself upward, and halfway up the fence his shoe touched a slender wire carefully woven through the fence links and behind him the sound of an alarm bell cut the night.

He shot a look over his shoulder. Lights going on in the facility, and in the corner of the building where the infirmary was located, some people moving quickly past the windows. And closer to him, coming out of the shadow darkness beneath the big tree, the long slender shape of the thing.

It was the thing that gave him the strength to climb the fence, the thing that gave him the push he needed up over the top, the thing that sent him falling, off-balance, into the damp grass.

He was up and running across the field, away from the facility, away from the flashlights already cutting across the lawn toward the gate, running the way he never ran in gym period, his legs pumping, arms driving, running through the slight tangle of bush and then climbing over a creaking barbed-wire fence. Across a roadway, up an embankment and toward the haunting one-eyed light of the approaching train.

He knew someone was helping him. He knew it wasn't

possible that he had managed, in pitch blackness, to come to the one place where the train had to slow down almost to a crawl. And he knew how you were supposed to do it; one of the mothers had worked at a place where you went in once or twice a week to talk to old people, and one of the old men had told him how he'd done it, how he'd gone back and forth across the country on a train without ever buying a ticket, and it was as if Peter himself had done it a hundred times.

He ran alongside the tracks and when the ladder-thing came toward him he just did it without thinking, just jumped and grabbed it, feeling the numbing jolt up both arms to the shoulder, just like the old man had said, and he did just what he'd been told, he hung on and kept his feet out of the way until the first jolt was gone, then he scrabbled up until his feet, too, were on the ladder. Press tight against the train car and move up to the roof without ever looking down or you'll get so dizzy you'll fall, and if you fall, that's it, sonny, you're minced. Don't ever ride on the roof in winter or when you're heading over the Rockies. But Peter didn't plan on heading over the Rockies and winter was gone for this year.

On top of the train car was a square ventilation box, the lid half open, and he held on to it tightly, one corner of his mind wondering what was in the car below: cows or pigs or things in boxes? He tried to look down inside, but it was dark, and when he raised himself the slightest bit he got dizzy and frightened, so he just lay flat on the roof, his hands hooked tightly to the ventilation box, his hair blowing in the wind, his nostrils burning with the fumes coming back from the diesel engine.

The little lights were still hovering around his head, but he couldn't hear the rasping noises for the takin'-off takin'-off of the wheels, the clicketyclackety gonna-go, gonna-go of the joints in the rails hitting against the big metal wheels. The lonesome moan of the diesel cut the night and he raised his head. Far down the tracks he saw lights. The old man had warned him about yard bulls and switch-house cops, so when the train started to slow, he did what the old man had told him to do, he moved carefully to the ladder and, face pressed against the still moving car, he made his way back down and waited until the train slowed enough that he could jump off and run behind a parked engine, flattening himself on the ground, peering through the jigsaw puzzle of wheels and undercarriages, looking for approaching legs and feet.

He was almost disappointed when he didn't see any. Still, it was a good game, better than anti-I-over or flag football, and he played it out exactly as the old man had told him. Move from car to car quickly, watching for the inspectors and bullyboys, then, when the coast is clear, run like hell away from the switchyards. Never mind where you're going, you can figure that out when you're away from the shunt yard and the CPR cops, who are the toughest in the whole country. Tougher even than Mounties, the old man had said disapprovingly.

The town was asleep. It was just like any other night when you can't sleep so you shinny out the window and prowl around wondering what kind of people live behind those windows, what kind of kids have bikes they leave outside where anybody could swipe them. Who owns all the dogs that come stiff-legged to the fences?

Lights coming around the corner ahead, and he ducked quickly into an alleyway, heart racing. He stood stockstill until the cruising police car had passed the alley and gone off down the street, and when the sound of its engine had faded away he raced down the alley, trying to ignore the dancing lights and the unmistakable buzzing sound.

He stopped at the gas station diner at the corner, raised himself on tiptoe and peered through the steamy window. A truck driver was having coffee and a piece of pie, talking and laughing with the waitress, and Peter was tempted to stay and lipread the conversation, but the dancing lights were growing in number and the insistent buzzing was becoming annoying, and he was afraid someone else might see the fireflies or hear the cricket-noise.

It was a chippertruck, the kind he had often seen going out to the pulp mill with loads of chips to be turned into paper. Somehow. He didn't know how. Just when his class was supposed to go out to the mill on a field trip, he'd been reassigned to a different foster home and had to change schools, so he missed out on learning how they took a zillion tons of wood chips and turned out paper for drawing and writing and finger-painting and putting on the wall in the bedroom.

There was a ladder up the back so the driver could spread his load and then arrange a canvas tarp over the top so the chips wouldn't blow all over the road. It wasn't easy going up the ladder. Like the one on the side of the train it went up straight so you had to almost lean backwards and take a lot of your weight on your arms. He wondered if that was how a fly felt going up a wall, straight up and down, and your leg muscles getting sore in a hurry.

The tarp wasn't pulled down tight: they never were, they would billow up with the wind as the truck rolled down the road, puffing up like bedsheets on a line. He squirmed and wriggled and managed to get himself under the tarp and safely into the aromatic chips inside. Only one or two of the firefly-lights got in with him and he hoped the others didn't hang around outside and make the trucker wonder whatinhell was going on up there. What if he came to check? What if he decided to tie his tarp down really tight and Peter couldn't get out and wound up made into paper himself?

He would have liked to have whistled, that was a good thing to do when you were scared, but he didn't want the trucker coming up to see why a load of chips was whistling, so he just sang songs to himself inside his head

hey ho my little horse
hey ho again sir
how many miles to Babylon
four score and ten sir
hey ho my little horse
hey ho again sir
can I get there by candlelight
you can and back again sir

that was a good one, and the mother who didn't have any more small boys, just big ones who were almost men, had sung it to him lots of times, sitting on a chair, holding him on her lap and jiggling her knees so it was like riding the little horse. Sometimes she held his hand and they skipped around the living room until they collapsed, laughing, on the carpet, and then she'd tickle him or blow on his neck until he yelled "uncle." He didn't know why he hadn't been able to stay there. She didn't get sick. He hadn't been bad. And she'd grabbed onto him when he left, grabbed onto him and squeezed him tight and kissed him. She'd said "It was nice having you with us, Peter. You're a good boy and I love you very much," and he'd wanted to ask why he had to leave, if that was true, but he didn't ask. Nobody ever told you anything anyway. And maybe there was a good reason, one he didn't know. Everybody always said Mind Your Own Business. Maybe it wasn't any of his business why he'd had to leave. Sometimes, at night, he sang the song inside his head and tried to remember what it was like to be jiggled and cuddled.

The big boys who were almost men would call him "short legs" and were always teasing him. They'd scoop him up and toss him over their shoulders and say "Hey, short legs, we'll never get there like that, hitch a ride," and they'd walk funny, deliberately bouncing up and down so he jiggled on their shoulders, lying bellydown, his laughter sounding funny as the jiggling made his breathing irregular.

They bought him ice cream cones and doubled him on their bikes. They didn't even mind if he tagged along and sat watching them at soccer practice, and if anybody asked who he was they'd shrug easily and say "He's the small sib," and he knew sib meant brother or sister.

He nearly jumped out of his skin when the truck roared to life. That was what was wrong with letting yourself remember things. He hadn't even heard the driver come out and get into the truck, hadn't even heard the door close. There were some bumps and some shakings, rumbles and roars and strange feelings as the gears changed several times and then they were rolling down the road, the smell of hemlock and fir strong in the air, the orange-tan tarp above like the sail of an old ship taking them to the places with weird names like the ones you sometimes heard in the late night movies on television, names like Baghdad and Cathay and Orinoco and

and at first he had hoped they would find out where he was living and show up on their big two-wheelers and say "Hey, small sib, want to go for a ride?" but they never showed up and when he got big enough to go looking for them, they were gone. He'd taken the bus into town, transferred to the other bus and got off at the right corner, and the house was there, but it wasn't the same, and he waited until he saw one of the people living in the house and when he didn't recognize that person at all he had just turned and headed back to the bus stop, wondering sadly where all the people went when they left his life.

When the truck went around a corner his body leaned into the chips, and when they went uphill he felt a gentle pressure against the rear of the box. He wanted very much to go to sleep, but he didn't dare in case he woke up being dumped into some kind of big pot in the place where they made all the paper. He wondered if it would hurt very much being boiled up into a soup of paperstuff. And would he be able to see what was going on in the room when he was part of the wallpaper on the wall? What if the chips beneath him opened up and he fell through to the bottom of the truck and then the chips closed over him and he smothered or was crushed? Would they find him? Would they know who he was or how he got there? Would they care?

He squirmed his way out from under the tarp, almost lost his balance in the sudden blast of wind rolling along the top of the canvas, grabbed at the ladder and began to inch his way down the steep metal rungs. Clinging to the bottom section of the ladder he watched the road slide away beneath the truck like a mottled grey and black ribbon or the back of some huge sinuous water-dwelling serpent. Wanting to let go, not daring to let go, feeling his terror return as the small dancing lights began to form a halo around his head, their twittering filling his ears with panic, he felt the truck slowing down to turn a corner, took a deep breath, hoped he wouldn't get broken and smashed, and flung himself sideways and away from the road toward the grass and bushes.

He hit the shoulder of the road with a thump, rolled, and slammed into a small bush that knocked the wind out of him in a great gasping whoosh. The truck disappeared down the road and Peter pulled himself to a sitting position, feeling his shoulder and arm where he had landed, feeling the rip in his shirt, knowing he had a big bruise starting on his hip.

He began to cry, great racking sobs coming up from his stomach, tightening his throat. Holding his injured arm, rocking with pain because the old man hadn't mentioned this part of it at all. Sobbing because he hadn't known about being alone in the darkness, being cold, with rips in your clothes, your skin itching with hemlock juice and a lump on your head where you hit a rock. He cried without knowing exactly why he cried. He cried because he was eleven years old and on his own in the black of night, knowing that somewhere behind him a thing was following his scent along the railroad tracks, two ugly heads searching, sniffing for a trace of Peter.

HE CROUCHED IN THE HUCKLEBERRY THICKET across the road from the milkstop and watched as the farmer and his shaggy dog headed back to the house, the dog jumping high and barking happily. He had crouched here for more than half an hour watching the farmer stack the shiny milk cans in a small cross between a rack and a shed, carefully stacking them in rows, talking to the dog as if he expected an answer. Once the dog had started across the road to investigate the smell of boy coming from the thicket, but the farmer had whistled softly and the dog had whirled and returned.

They went up the steps and across the porch and entered the house, the door closing behind them. Peter knew they would probably have breakfast now; he imagined huge hunks of ham and two or three eggs, maybe even some pancakes and toast with big gobs of strawberry jam. His mouth watered and his belly rumbled.

He crept out of the thicket carrying a battered and rusty tin can in his hand. It wasn't easy, but he managed to pry off the lid on one of the big milk cans. He scooped up a canful of milk and drank it in great eager gulps. A few flecks of rust from the old can floated on top of the thick white milk and he reached in with a grimy finger, flicking the rust specks into the ditch. Another can of milk and the pain in his belly went away and the shaky feeling left his legs. He drank until he couldn't hold any more, then refilled the rusty can, put the lid on the milk can, and headed across the road to the ditch. He had no more than settled himself to sip the rest of the milk slowly, than he heard the sound of an approaching truck.

He crouched in the thicket, watching through the viny tangle as the driver, whistling softly to himself, swung full cans up on the truck and left empty ones in their place. Peter grinned and wondered if the man noticed that one of the cans was lighter than the others and the lid not down as solidly. He sipped the stolen milk and waited until the driver got in his truck and drove away, and when the sound of the engine had faded and died, Peter walked along the ditch, occasionally sipping milk, until the can was empty and he threw it away in a thicket of blossoming blackberry vines.

It was too early for berries, and even if he had known how to set a snare to catch a rabbit he didn't know if there were wild rabbits to be caught. Or what to do with it if he did catch one.

He wasn't sure he could use a rock to kill it. Or anything else to kill it. And if he did kill it, he knew he couldn't eat it raw, and he had no way of lighting a fire.

His arm was sore and after he'd walked a bit his hip started aching and he limped until his good leg was tired and sore too. He didn't dare ask anybody for anything; as soon as they saw a lone boy, dirty, limping and hungry, they would call the police.

He slept that night under a tree, shivering and weeping, and almost wishing he was back at the facility. The ground beneath him was cold as the night damp rose and seeped through his clothes to his skin. His sore hip throbbed and stiffened, the bark of the tree against which he was leaning bit into his skin and his fingers were so cold it didn't even do any good to tuck his hands in his armpits and cuddle himself.

The following day he had nothing but water, and he didn't sleep at all that night; his belly was aching and it was too cold to even cry. He tried curling up in a ball, but it wasn't warm and finally he started walking again, not because there was any place he wanted to go, but because he just couldn't stand to stay there, shaking and shivering and crying. He walked through the dark bush, wondering what was making the noises in the underbrush, walking and crying, not caring where he was going as long as it was away, far away.

AFTERNOON, AND THE SUN WAS WARM. It shone through the branches and the budding overhead and though the ground was damp, it wasn't cold. He lay down in the sun, glad the hunger pains were gone from his stomach, wondering where they had gone, and why. The breeze barely ruffled his uncombed hair, and within moments he was asleep, the warm afternoon sun easing the ache in his muscles.

It was the cricket-sound that woke him up again. At first he thought it was the chitter of birds in the trees, but then he knew it was this other, the thing he couldn't name. He sat up, looking around wildly, and the grove was full of dancing lights. The firefly-lightning bug things had found him again and there were more of them than there ever had been.

He crouched, ready to run down the path, but then they all moved in that direction and he hesitated, wondering if they were going to follow him or attack him. Then, coming down the very path he had been going to take, slithering along relentlessly, the thing with two heads. Every time he saw it, it seemed a different size. Right now it was very small, and if you didn't know better you'd think it was just an ordinary snake, but it was travelling with incredible speed.

He whirled and ran away from it, away from the dancing lights and cricket noises, running blindly, ignoring the branches that slapped his face, stumbling over roots and vines, running, hoping the lights wouldn't be able to keep up with him. Every time the lights found him the snake-thing found him.

He broke out of the bushland and stopped suddenly. Ahead of him a beach, some rocks and pebbles, a clutter of bleached logs and some sticks and kelp, and then miles and miles and miles of sea shining in the sunlight. He wished he could run on top of the water, jumping from one wavetip to another until he got someplace that wouldn't allow lights, or noises, or snakes, or anything. If the snake-thing came there was no place to go: he couldn't go back—the thing waited down the path; he couldn't go forward because he couldn't run on top of the water. On either side the beach stretched invitingly for a distance, but then the rocks and sand seemed to disappear into the water, as if this curved half-oval of beach were the last place in the world, with nothing else beyond it except water, and behind him the unnamed threat that had chased him for what seemed all of his life.

He was out of breath and dizzy, his legs shaking, so he sat down quickly on a barnacled rock, but his back began to ache so he moved to sit on the sand and lean against a giant weather-whitened log, hiding from the lights, hiding from the snake, playing with some shells and pebbles, letting his fingers feel the ridges and whorls. He stared down at the dry white half-shell and something stirred in his memory. He rose and began to look for shells that weren't empty, the ones with the edible animal still living inside.

He collected several oysters and tried desperately to hammer one of them open with a large rock. He could chip the fluted edges easily enough, but when he tried to bash through the thick end, the end where the muscle was, the muscle just tightened up even more and the shell stayed firmly shut. He was panting, almost weeping in his frustration.

"By the time you get her open, boy, she won't be fit to eat." The voice came from nowhere, and Peter jumped up, terrified.

3

PETER STARED, FROZEN. An old man was watching him from the top of the bank, a man so incredibly old you couldn't even begin to guess when he'd been young. His face was lined and seamed, his eyes nearly hidden in wrinkles. His hair was long and thin and blew every whichway at the whim of the breeze. Several of the dancing lights were near his head but there was no suggestion of the nerve-racking noises.

Peter dropped the oyster, whirled, and ran slapbang into a very large, sober-featured man with burning eyes. He tried to dodge, but the man just reached out, grabbed him without hurting him and, as if Peter were a parcel, tucked him under his arm and walked back to where the old man stood behind the forgotten pile of unshucked oysters.

The old man reached into his pocket and brought out a clasp knife. He did it so fast and so well Peter wasn't even able to see what he did. The oyster lay open on his gnarled brown hand, held out invitingly.

"Me, I like 'em better with fixin's," he remarked to nobody in particular, handing the oyster to Peter. "Take 'em and dip 'em in beatup egg, then roll 'em in bread crumbs or cracker crumbs or a bit'a cornmeal if you got it. Fry 'em in melted margarine with some onion and squirt 'em with a bit'a vinegar . . . half a dozen like that and a bit'a potata maybe, and I wouldn't call the Queen'a England my cousin. But if she come to lunch, she'd eat'em too, I betcha!"

What the old man was describing sounded a lot better than what Peter was tasting, and swallowing the oyster was beginning to feel a lot like trying to be sick. Finally it went down, and as he got the aftertaste of salt and seaweed, he shuddered, swallowing again quickly.

"That's what I thought," the old man said, satisfied. "A raw oyster is somethin' you gotta swalla two or three times to get where it's goin'. Fella told me once that there's rich people pay good money to eat raw oysters. Me, I don't see any sense in it. Raw oysters is for gulls and ravens and things as don't have stoves. Us, we got a fire, and fryin' pans and vinegar, and taters and lotsa coffee, don't make sense to go back to livin' like a gull."

He talked strangely, as if his top and bottom teeth never left each other, his bottom jaw barely moving at all. All the "p" sounds flew out of his mouth like little birds, but the "s" sounds seemed reluctant to leave his mouth at all. "G" sounded almost like "c" or maybe "k." Vinegar sounded more like finniker and gull sounded almost like kull.

"Tell ya what, boy, if you help him gather up some we'll take'em home and cook'em up right for you." The old man made a head gesture in the direction of the silent man.

Peter stared for a moment; the silent man just waited, neither smiling nor frowning, just waiting.

"Oh, don't have ta worry," the old man chattered easily, "we won't keep ya do ya decide ya wants to leave." His chuckle rolled up from his belly, his face fell into folds and wrinkles like an accordion. "And we're more used ta eatin' oysters than ta eatin' boys; boys're too tough anyway, I bet."

Peter felt silly then. Standing dithering, obviously hungry

but unwilling to make a move toward helping gather some lunch. If they'd been going to kill him they'd have done it when the old man whipped open the knife. The silent man could have smashed his head in with a rock or snapped his neck. Peter moved to a large rock where the oysters were hanging ready to be pried off, but the silent man touched his arm, shook his head and pointed to another rock, still in water even though the tide was out. They took off their shoes and waded into the water, moving to the half-submerged rock, and began to pry off the tightly clinging shells. Peter would have taken them all, but the silent man shook his head no, made a gesture with his hands, and started walking back to the beach. With nothing else to do, Peter followed.

"Some folks take'em home shell and all," the old man chattered away, and Peter wondered where the story had got started that Indians were hard to talk to. "Us, we always had the villages close to the sea, so it didn't much matter, I suppose, but even then we shucked'em where we got'em. You see, every oyster shell, she's got seeds on her for oh, maybe six, maybe seven other oysters. Take'em home and you've killed a half a dozen and only got one to eat. But shuck'em and chuck'em and there'll always be oysters to eat." He threw a handful of shells back into the sea, the inner shell glittering in the sunlight. "This way, we put back the shell and the seeds and the seeds grow into oysters. That's howcum you see'em growing in bunches, a big one and a whole buncha smaller ones. Three, four years from now won't be no way at all to know we grabbed us a big feast here."

Peter lobbed his shell; it arced from his hand, caught a gust of wind and rode like a frisbee, spinning down yards from shore.

"That's a good one," the old man remarked, approvingly.

"Oysters like deep water. I didn't think a city fella like you would know that, but I guess you showed me somethin'." He put the last oyster in the plastic cottage cheese container, handed it to the silent man, then got slowly to his feet. "Always wash off oyster-slime in the sea," he muttered. "Some say ya do it to say thank-you, but I think it's because the salt cuts the slime better'n fresh water will."

"You kill slugs with salt," Peter blurted suddenly, surprising himself. "Slugs are sort of . . . slushy . . . like oysters . . . and if you put salt down they sort of crawl over it and then they just . . . melt."

"Why'd you want to do that? Kill slugs? You don't eat'em do you?"

"No, but they eat the garden," Peter explained, feeling his face go all red the way it always did if someone asked him a direct question. He could feel the stutter starting, too, the one that made everyone so sure he was telling lies. "They g-g-get on the l-l-leaves, and they l-l-leave holes a-and . . ." He came to a jerky halt, hoping the old man wouldn't think he was making it all up to get attention.

"So that's what does it," the old man laughed, "and here's me all this time blamin' the ladybugs. Slugs." He looked at the silent man, and there was an instant communication with their eyes as if other things were being said besides the things the old man was saying to Peter. "Well, now, we'll just pick us up some salt when we go into town and we'll keep them buggers offa the lettuce this year. Slugs, huh? Well, they've et the last cabbage they're gonna get. Salt'em."

They walked along the beach, then angled off through the woodland. Peter was frightened, darting glances constantly, watching to see if the snake-thing was following.

The old man watched the boy's eyes constantly darting, searching the underbrush, looking for danger. He looked up, knew He Who Would Sing had seen the same signs of fear. He Who Would Sing spoke with his hands and the old man nodded quietly.

He felt sad watching the boy. Such a little boy, even younger than He Who Would Sing had been when he arrived so many years ago, his face bruised, his front tooth chipped, his body marked and sore. How many children did this make? How many children had come to him in his lifetime?

He had been a child himself when the first one found him. Charlie Jack, who lived with his uncle and a woman not the wife of the uncle. Charlie Jack had had marks on his back from a leather belt and a bruise on his face from a heavy fist and he was hungry. So he had taken him home and his father had fed them both, then had gone to see the uncle of Charlie Jack and after that Charlie Jack had lived with him and had been his brother. But Charlie Jack was dead now, and so was the wife of Charlie Jack and both of their children. Dead of a sickness they said had come from the millions of dead bodies left behind when the white man fought his big war. A long time ago, and the memory of Charlie Jack was as fresh as it had been at the time he was lifted into the burial tree, but the pain of the memory was gone now.

And after Charlie Jack there was the baby whose mother had got her from a slanty-eyed fisherman who had come to catch herring and who went away never knowing he had left a baby inside the woman who had laughed with him. The mother didn't want the baby because the new man said there was no place for a baby on his boat, not a slanty-eyed baby that wasn't his. And so he had asked if he could have the baby. The mother had laughed and said What do you want with a baby, what do you expect to do with a baby? I will give her to my mother, he had said, and that is what he had done, and the baby had been his sister. They gave her a name that meant Dearly Loved and she had grown tall and learned to dance and laugh and had married a young man from Nootka and had ten children. She and her husband were buried at Nootka now, and the children had children and grandchildren. Others had come into his life until it was said in the village that he could find a child where others couldn't find a fish.

And now this one, who was not of the people but who had need.

He Who Would Sing touched the boy on the shoulder, then pointed upwards, but the boy didn't know where to look.

"On the tree," the old man said softly. "See him walkin' up the tree . . . big woodpecker . . . he walks around the tree in an upgoin' spiral, and he sees every inch of that tree, every bug, every hole that might hide a bug. See him?"

"Why doesn't he fly away?" the boy asked.

"Why should he? I'm not gonna hurt him. You're not gonna hurt him. *He* ain't gonna hurt him. Why would the pecker fly away from those who aren't gonna hurt him?"

"How does he know we aren't going to hurt him?"

"Oh, he knows."

They walked on through the woods and down the meadow to where the cabin waited in the sunlight. Whatever it was the boy was afraid of, it seemed it might come from the underbrush or it might fall from a tree, it might come out from behind a bush or it might even fly at him, because he searched all levels from ground to sky, his eyes darting constantly, his fingers clenching and unclenching nervously.

PETER HESITATED AT THE DOOR OF THE CABIN, letting the two who lived here enter first. The old man smiled, made an inviting gesture with his hand, and Peter walked in, keeping close to the door, unsure of himself and suddenly very shy.

One long room, and at the back a curtain hanging over what was probably a doorway to a second room. The end of the big room nearest the door was dominated by a large black woodstove. On the end wall to his right, several cupboards and a sink and counter with no real tap but rather a small hand pump securely screwed to the counter above the sink. A large table, four wooden chairs, an enormous wood box three-quarters full of split wood and, to his left, a fabulous clutter and collection of strange forms and shapes.

Carved masks, totem poles, statues, wall plaques, strange faces—not quite animal, not quite human—and, arranged over the back of a sagging sofa, a blanket. But what a blanket. Almost as big as a bunk bed blanket, deep blue with a red border seven or eight inches wide and in the middle, bright against the deep blue, a bird with a sort of horn on his head, a bird with sequin feathers, a sequin beak, his sequin eye staring, glittering in the sunlight coming through the window. Peter's feet moved him across the room to touch the bird. His hands itched to touch the bird, itched so much he jammed both hands in his pockets; he mustn't touch, it wasn't his, you didn't touch anything that wasn't yours. And still the bird beckoned.

The silent man was getting everything ready for the meal and the old man was helping, watching Peter's reactions closely. He smiled as the boy was drawn toward the blanket and when Peter shoved his hands roughly in his pockets the old man exchanged a long glance with the silent man, then put aside the dishes he was placing on the table and moved toward the boy.

"That's my dance cape," he offered gently. Peter stared from the blanket to the old man, then back to the blanket.

"You never seen a dance cape before?" the old man continued. Peter shook his head, his eyes glued to the sequined bird. The old man reached out, took the blanket and draped it over his shoulders, the bird wings outstretched across his back, the bird eye glittering happily, expectantly. "Watch his face. He loves to dance, this bugger," and the old man began to move, stiffly, slowly, his legs shuffling, his body making formal centuries-old calculated half-turns and dips. The bird seemed to soar the heavens, his glittering eye watching the world below, soaring and swooping, his sequin feathers shivering in the breeze. Peter felt dizzy, as if he too was flying high above the mountains and streams.

"You like that." The old man was pleased and Peter nodded, wishing he could say something. "When I was your age there was a man from Hesquiath could dance until you could see the blackfish jumpin' out of the waves and shakin' water offa his back in the sunlight." He placed the dance cape back on the sofa, smoothing its folds gently. "Me, I used to dance and dance. Me and Eagle Flies High here, we'd dance all night and never get tired. Sometimes the parties'd go on for three or four days and we'd still be dancin' strong at the end. Not no more, though." He slapped his dry twig handy legs with the flat of his hand. "These fellers got just about all they can do to walk me from place to place, never you mind dancin'."

A low whistle from the mute man at the stove, and the old

man turned. The silent man's face was suddenly cut by a wide, happy grin, his fingers danced and the old man laughed.

"He's bein' dirty again," he chuckled happily. "He says there's other things I used to do that I can't do no more. Don't pay much attention to him when he gets like that, he likes to be silly. Thinks he's a joker, he does."

The fingers flashed again, the old man chuckled and the silent man went back to peeling potatoes and beating eggs.

"He's gotta have the last word," the old man announced, moving to sit on the sofa with Peter. He gestured to the blanket and the glittering bird. "That fella there, Eagle Flies High, there's a story about him. From the Before times. The Storm Wind had a daughter, called Storm Daughter, and she was just about the most beautiful woman around these parts at that time. Dark, she was, with fierce storm-eyes and wild storm-hair and teeth as white as the froth on the waves. Well, she saw Eagle Flies High way up in the sky, floating on the breeze and falling through the air to catch fish in his claws. She thought he was just about the most perfect thing she'd ever seen and she loved him. She was the daughter of the Storm Wind and he figured whatever she wanted she could have, so he huffed him up the most almighty storm we ever had on this coast and he blew Eagle Flies High far and wide until he landed him on the beach where Storm Daughter was waiting. She did magic on him and he just stared at her and was happy to stay right where Storm Wind blew him to. They lived together and as things always have a way of seeming to happen, Storm Daughter, she got herself a baby from him. It was a boy, half human and half bird, and for a long time she carried him in a pack on her back because he hadn't learned neither to walk nor to fly. But the Wanton Wind, she got a bit jealous of the happiness going down on that stretch of beach and she started blowing in Eagle Flies High's ear, telling him of the tall cliffs and the free spaces, telling him of the waves and the blackfish, the clouds and the sky. Well, Storm Wind, he got angry about all this interferin' and he started to jaw it up with Wanton Wind and they got themselves into the usual kind of stupidity all folks get into when they're mad and unreasonable and between the two of 'em, didn't they blow up a wind that picked Eagle Flies High offa the beach and blew him right back where he come from, only further. Storm Daughter, she cried and she give the sharp side'a her tongue to botha them; Storm Wind and Wanton Wind got the news, you can be sure'a that. Storm Daughter, she turned into Wild Woman of the Forest, and she started singin' a sad song that you can sometimes hear in the trees at night. A song about strong wings, the race of strong wings, the challenge of strong wings and the wind that can always defeat the wings. And she's still lookin' for a song to sing for her son, because he's not bird nor man and he's not wind nor storm, he's a star now, and he'll stay one until his mother can find him a name and a song. And that on my cape, that's Eagle Flies High; the only thing that can keep him from going where he wants to go is the wind. It's maybe one of the most powerful things going and nobody ever seen it. Somethin' to think about, ain't it? Rocks are strong and thunder is powerful, but the wind can wear a rock away to a pebble and the wind can blow the thunder right off over the hill. But ya can't see it." He smiled, looked around, slapped his hand on his bandy leg. "By golly, he's got'er all done in the time we been jawin', if we don't hurry us up he'll turt'er outside for the ravens!"

They sat at the table, Peter's hands and face freshly scrubbed, his hair wet and palmed flat to his head. A platter of golden fried oysters, another platter of hash brown potatoes, some sliced tomatoes and the nose-tingling scent of fresh coffee. Peter folded his hands on his lap and waited, his throat moving often, swallowing the saliva that gathered in his mouth. He felt shaky again and close to tears. The old man began to hand the platter to the boy and Peter hesitated, afraid he'd do something dumb like he usually did, maybe drop it or spill it. Something in the boy's face spoke to the old man and he filled the waiting plate, then passed the platter to the silent man. Peter was glad the old man hadn't handed him the platter. It was always like that, a person would hand him something and he'd be sure he had a good grip on it and then all of a sudden there it was, all over the floor and everyone mad at him again.

He waited until everyone had their serving, waited until the older men had started to eat, then he carefully spread his paper napkin on his lap and, with trembling hands, picked up his knife and fork. What he wanted to do was just eat, just grab it and stuff it into his mouth, it looked and smelled so good, but it isn't proper to do things that way.

The silent man watched from the corner of his eye and the old man watched frankly as Peter very carefully moved his coffee cup to where there was no chance of it getting spilled. With careful and precise movements he arranged things Just So, and when it was all to his satisfaction he began to eat his meal, carefully cutting the oysters into small pieces, his hands actually shaking with repressed hunger. He hoped nobody would notice he wasn't chewing each piece as often as he should. He couldn't. He didn't care if he did get a bellyache, the best his tongue and throat would let him do was thirteen or fourteen chews each piece and then they forced him to swallow.

"You got good table manners, boy," the old man said quietly, smiling gently. "Someone spent a lot of time teaching you good manners like that."

Peter carefully put his knife and fork in the proper place on his plate, chewed and swallowed carefully before speaking. "I lived in a place once where they said if you couldn't eat properly, you wouldn't eat at all. They said if you insisted on eating like an animal you could sit in the dark closet and go without your meal until you knew better." When nobody replied to his explanation, he again picked up his knife and fork and mechanically went back to eating his meal.

The mute stared at Peter, then rose suddenly and stood in the doorway for a few moments, his hands clenched and angry and his back stiff. Then he went to the cupboard and brought out a loaf of homemade bread, cut some thick slices and placed them invitingly close to Peter's plate. He went to the stove and got the coffee pot, filled the old man's cup again, then returned the pot to the stove and refilled Peter's plate.

When they had all eaten as much as they could and the old man was sitting over his third cup of coffee, Peter managed a small smile and a hesitant nod. "That was very good," he said carefully. "Thank you very much."

"We thank you," the old man replied. "It isn't every day we get a chance to have company, nor every day we get a chance to meet someone new. Mostly we just have to put up with each other. We get along good, but He Who Would Sing, he doesn't talk much."

The silent man grinned, began to clear the table, and the old man noticed how quickly the boy moved to help. He carefully stacked the dishes on the counter near the unfinished sink, then looked around puzzled, wondering how anybody could use a sink that had no drainpipe. He Who Would Sing reached under the counter, brought out a chipped enamel basin, put in a handful of powdered soap, then added water from the steaming kettle on the old black stove. He added a dipper of cold water from the bucket near the pump, tested it with his hand, added another dipper of cold water, tested again, and nodded.

"I'll do them," the boy said quietly, and He Who Would Sing flashed his broad grin, bowing from the waist and gesturing with his hand that the sink and the dishes were the boy's own domain.

Peter first washed, rinsed and dried all the cutlery, putting things away in the places from which he had seen them taken. Then the cups, then the plates, then the platters and finally the heavy black frying pans. He wiped the table and countertop, folded the dishtowel and hung it in place with the others behind the stove, then wrung out the dishcloth and hung it to dry, too. Then he stared, puzzled, at the basin of water and the sink that had no drainpipe.

"We just chuck it outside," the old man said softly. "That's how come we use powdered soap insteada detergent." The silent man grinned, took the basin as far as the door and tossed the water in a briefly rainbowing arc into the yard.

"Doesn't he talk at all?" Peter asked hesitantly.

"Can't talk, boy," the old man answered evenly.

Peter flashed a quick look at He Who Would Sing and the big man placed his fingers on his throat, then shook his head and made gestures with his hands.

"He can't talk," the old man repeated. "He never has and he never will. Doctor says there's something missing in his throat. Born that way, I guess. We went to a whole buncha doctors about it. For a while about all we did with ourselves was go to doctors, but they all said the same thing so we kinda figured we might's well just give'er up as a bad job. One of them said that inside'a your throat there's a sort of a box thing, and he said as how when you talk you're actually playin' on this box like playin' on a musical instrument. Only he hasn't got all the things in his throat that he needs and his voice box never got finished getting made."

"Not any sounds at all?" Peter gasped.

"Oh, he can make a funny sort of noise when he's laughin', but it isn't really a Sound, it's the air coming out in a sort of a huff huff. And he can kinda cough if he's got a cold, but it wouldn't wake nobody up at night. He talks with his fingers. And there's times," the old man added dryly, "that his hands don't shut up from dawn to dark."

"I'm sorry your son can't talk," Peter said, hoping nobody would think him impertinent.

"Oh, he ain't my son. I'm his throat and he's my strength. We get along pretty good, him and me. When he first come I wasn't old and puny like I am now, see, so I could teach him all the things I knew and now that I'm too old to do'em, he does'em for me."

"I thought he was your son. Most old men have got sons."

"Oh, he's my son now, right enough." The old man had already learned not to address himself directly to the boy. Peter quickly became uneasy if both words and gaze were directed at him, so the old man looked at the stove and talked to the boy. "He showed up here a long time ago; he was maybe sixteen or seventeen but already built as big as most men. Been in some kinda trouble in town, somethin' to do with booze and a woman and punchin' in some feller's face; usual sorta story showed up here in the middle of the night all beat up and he just stayed with me. We learned to talk with finger signs and we adopted each other Indian-style and here we be."

"Did the police come after him?"

"No, they never did." The old man settled himself more comfortably on his chair. "Never saw hide nor hair nor stripe nor gun of them and when we go into town nobody bothers us. I don't think he's Indian himself," the old man mused, as if the thought had entered his head for the first time. "He didn't know nothin' about it when he got here, but he's kinda darkish. I guess he is now, though, living here with me like he does."

"What's his name?"

"Well, there's some folks call him Loony, they figure if he don't speak he's a few bricks short of a load and not all at home upstairs. But the name he got when he became a dancer, that's his spirit name. Comes from your biggest dream or your biggest gift. And he got the name He Who Would Sing."

"What's your special name?"

"Me? Oh, I got me a whole raft of names, boy. I had me one name when I was just a baby and then I got me another one when I started walkin' around bein' bad like boys are. When I got a few whiskers on my chin I got another name and then I traded some stuff for a name and . . . I got me lotsa names. What's yours?"

"Peter. My name is Peter. Peter Baxter."

"Well, Peter, we kinda figured we'd maybe just spend the day doin' nothin'. Thought we'd maybe pretend we were rich and lazy."

A quick whistle, the flashing of the fingers and the gleaming smile.

"He says," the old man translated as the mute made a snapping gesture with his hands, then let his head loll comically, "he says insteada bein' broke and lazy like we really are. Think you'd like to join us in doin' that?"

"Yes, sir, I'd like that," Peter nodded.

"Did you know that the name Peter means a rock? Didn't know that, huh? Well it does. Don't know where it comes from, but that's what it means. Not just a rock you hold in your hand, the big kind you build with. Ever seen people build with rock? Them eyetalians is good at it, they can bust a big rock with a sledge and by golly if it don't fit just right where it's supposed to. Now if you two'll just give me a hand outta this chair we'll take us out in the sunshine a bit. Get us a good tan." And he laughed softly to himself about something.

They sat on the steps in the warming sun and listened to the breeze in the evergreens. The boy eyed the carving area, the figures standing against the wall of the cabin, the bench that used to be a log, the seat that used to be a stump.

"Wood's nice," the old man said to nobody in particular. "Not just for lookin' at but for feelin' and smellin', for touchin' and listenin' to. Some people think there's a trick to carvin', they think you've got to *make* something that wasn't there before, but that's just startin' at the arsend and working forward, what you do is start with what's already there. Everything you could ever imagine is in every piece'a wood and all you got to do is take away what ya don't need and what you were lookin' for is there. No big secret to it at all. 'Course," he added with a grin, "it takes some practice."

Peter moved to the carving bench, sat down and stared at the tools. Then he picked up a piece of wood and felt it, tapped it, even smelled it. But it didn't seem that the wood was talking to him, and after a few minutes he put it down and laid his head on the workbench. The sun warmed his face, his hair blew in the wind and almost immediately, he was asleep.

The silent one flashed his fingers, the old man nodded, staring off at the memories he never fully shared with anyone.

"Yeah," he answered with a nod, "he's in trouble sure enough. Poor little bugger, he's been runnin' a long time." He watched the moving fingers. "'Course he's half crazy. Who ain't? If I wasn't half crazy I'd never be bothered with you and if you weren't half crazy you'd never be bothered with me. As it is we're both so crazy we can even talk to each other and think we understand what we're talkin' about."

The mute rose from the steps and walked away slowly, hands thrust deep into his pockets. He remembered very little of his life before he had come here. He had never tried to remember, as if he preferred not to have existed before this place. He knew he had always been able to hear, but he couldn't remember a time when he had been able to speak. He had the feeling that even as a baby his crying had been silent. The old man told him often that his throat made sounds but the sounds could only be heard in that other reality, that other plane of life so few people knew existed. He wasn't sure he liked the idea of his voice being heard in the spirit world; if he felt lonely in this world without his voice, his voice probably felt lonely in the spirit world with no body.

People had tried to be nice to him. He could remember, if he tried. He could remember his parents trying hard to hide the puzzlement in their eyes, trying hard not to let him know how much his handicap hurt them, how they were reminded each time someone else's child laughed that their child's laughter would never be heard. He had always known they loved him, but he had always known a feeling of failure, as if somehow it was his fault that he had been born imperfect.

The old man said this was a sign of Specialness. All the Special feel alienated. All souls live in that other plane, and sometimes when a soul leaves the spirit world to live in this world, the trip is incomplete. Perhaps the soul is in too big a hurry to get here, or perhaps there was a reason for coming incomplete.

The old man had explained carefully that some people were still in touch with the spirits. You could tell a lot about people by watching how they treated the Different Ones. In the old days if a child came with a hare-shorn lip or a club-twisted foot, it wasn't a terrible thing or a hurtful thing; it meant the child's soul was still in touch with the spirit world. If someone talked to himself he wasn't "crazy," he wasn't even talking to himself, he was talking to the spirits and it wasn't his fault if the rest of the people couldn't see and hear the spirits, it wasn't his fault if the rest of the people were incapable.

He'd gone to school and learned to read, but he couldn't read out loud like the other children, so he was never really sure if he was reading what was written on the page or what he thought was written on the page. He could write; for a long time he had written messages on slips of paper, trying to communicate, but

but that was a long time ago. That was before someone had laughingly given him a few drinks from a brown bottle, before the woman with the red lips and soft skin had laughed and asked him if he could dance, before

before things started getting confused and everyone was pulling at him, and he tried to write an explanation but the men didn't want to read any notes; one of them slapped the pencil and notepaper away and called him Dummy and then he was hitting out, only it wasn't the man who had called him Dummy who got it, it was a police, and people were running away from him, frightened, and two more police were coming. The woman was crying and saying Stop it, please, he didn't *do* anything, but nobody was listening to her. He knew his face was bleeding and he knew nobody would give him a chance to write notes to explain he hadn't meant to hit the police

and so he ran. He ran and they chased him until he lost them in the dark bush. He had fallen several times, and he was sure sounds had come from his throat, pain sounds and fear sounds, he was sure that if they had only stopped making noise themselves they'd have heard him screaming Leave me alone, I haven't done anything wrong, but even though he Knew what his voice would sound like, even though he Knew . . .

He tried to tell the old man he had heard his own voice that night. The old man nodded and said Yes, probably you did. If part of you is in the spirit world then you'll be in touch with the spirit world so you'll be able to hear your voice. He wanted to ask if the old man could hear his voice; the old man was in touch with the spirit world. But he was afraid to ask, afraid the old man would say No, he couldn't hear the spirit voice. If the old man couldn't hear it, maybe it wasn't in the spirit world. Maybe he had no voice at all.

It wasn't true that he had found this place. The old man had found him. He had crashed through the thick undergrowth and fallen, and it was just too hard to get up again, his head was spinning, his face was bleeding, he hurt . . .

And then this wrinkled face was inches from his own, strong brown hands were raising him from the damp moss and leaves, and the old man half carried him to the cabin.

When he woke up he was lying on an old couch, the dried blood washed from his hands and face. The bruises on his body were sore but the hurt that had always been inside him was gone.

Now there was a boy sleeping with his head resting on his arms, his arms resting on the carving block. A young boy with an unruly shock of brown-blond hair, a boy who was so frightened He Who Would Sing could see fear vibrations coming from him, could smell the fear rising from him.

He Who Would Sing had never had a son. He had no idea what to do, no idea how a parent would treat a frightened child, no idea what to say even if he could speak. He looked back at the small cabin, at the ancient man watching over the sleeping boy, and he knew the only thing he could do was treat the boy as he himself had once been treated. In that moment he also knew the old man, alone, would never be able to help the boy. The old man needed help to look after himself, now. He Who Would Sing was needed.

He walked back toward the small cabin, lay on the grass and stared up at the springtime sky. Waiting.

SUPPER WAS THICK STEW SERVED OVER MASHED POTATOES, homemade bread with margarine, and coffee, and for dessert there were berries from the previous summer, preserved in a quart glass bottle. Peter moved quietly to the table, waited until the others were seated, then sat himself on the old wooden chair. He checked to be sure his knife, fork, and spoon were correctly positioned, moved his coffee cup to where it wouldn't get accidentally bumped by his elbow, and again remembered the mother who had shown him that if you put things where Nothing Can Go Wrong, nothing will go wrong, there won't be accidents with the milk and everyone angry, there won't be forks falling to the floor or bread falling butter-side-down and a mess to be wiped clean.

When the old man and the silent one were eating, the boy picked up his knife and fork. He began to eat slowly and carefully, chewing rhythmically.

"You don't talk much, do you boy," the old man said suddenly.

Peter finished his mouthful of food, swallowed, put down his knife and fork. "No sir. Children are supposed to be seen and not heard. One of the fathers told me you don't speak unless you're spoken to."

He Who Would Sing scraped his chair back angrily and moved to glare out the door. Peter blinked, stared down at his plate.

"What's the matter, boy?"

"Is he mad at me?"

"Him? You don't know him very well yet, that's all." The old man reached for a piece of bread and calmly spread margarine on it. "If ever he gets mad at you he'll do a lot more than go to the door like that."

The mute moved back to the table, shrugged, and sat down to continue to eat. "You ever seen anybody shout with his hands?" the old man asked, eating and talking easily. "One time he was so mad he thumped his fist down on the table and all the cups jumped like they was scared. Another time he stomped his foot. We had an orange-coloured cat living with us that time and when he stomped that cat lit out like his tail was on fire. Stayed gone two days. Does he ever get mad at you, maybe that's what he'll do. Sometimes he claps them big hands'a his together and it sounds like a board bein' broke. When he first come here, when he was younger, I had a helluva time with his feet. He'd kick things with'em, and he's got big feet. So one day he hauled off and he kicked at the wall, and me I just whirled around and I yelled right in his face."

The gigantic mute nodded, grinning with the memory; then he opened his mouth and for a moment Peter was sure he could hear laughter, deep, full-throated from-the-belly laughter. Then the large brown fingers flashed and Peter looked inquiringly at the old man.

"Oh, him," the old man snorted sarcastically. "He's tellin' you I yap a lot." He drank his coffee thoughtfully. "Well, maybe I do. 'Course you gotta take into consideration, I gotta talk for two. You ever try arguin' both sides of a question at the same time? You should try it sometimes. But then, I forgot, you don't talk much."

"I do when I have something to say," Peter blurted.

"Just as well. Nobody listens anyway. He don't. Don't pay attention to a thing I say." The silent one whistled sharply, made a gesture with both hands as if rubbing a huge belly, then put his tongue between his lips and blew sharply. Peter's eyes widened at the power of the rude sound.

"He says I'm fulla hot air," the old man interpreted. The mute shook his head, repeated the rude sound. Peter put down his knife and fork, swallowed carefully. "I don't think he means hot air," he said shyly, and the mute laughed happily, his face glowing, his soundless throat swelling.

"You're right," the old man said gravely, "but I didn't want to use bad language in front of a gentleman with good manners."

When supper was finished, Peter cleared and wiped the table and put away the margarine, salt, pepper, sugar and bread. Then, carefully stacking everything in its proper order, he did the dishes. There was a certain way to do them, the father had said sternly, and you might as well learn the right way from the beginning. The cleanest things first, the dirtiest and greasiest things last, and if the water gets too greasy, empty it and start with fresh. But do it properly or you'll just wind up doing it again.

The two friends got out a deck of cards and a cribbage board and started to play. Peter had seen people playing cards before, and one place he'd stayed he'd played Snap and Old Maid with the foster brothers, so he watched out of the corner of his eye while he did the dishes.

"Fifteen two, fifteen four and a pair makes eight," the old man intoned, moving his peg. A sharp whistle and the mute held up six fingers, his head shaking. "Oh well," the old man muttered, caught, moving his peg back two holes, "she worked once."

Peter wanted to ask the old man why he was cheating. But then he saw the mute deliberately sneak his peg ahead three holes.

"Here, you bugger, I saw that," the old man snapped, his eyes twinkling, belying the tone of his voice. "Think I don't know? That's how come you always win. Always doing that." And his mumbling continued long after the mute had shrugged and replaced his peg.

When the dishes were finished, the water emptied, the towel carefully hung away, everything done properly, the boy moved to the battered old couch, watching the crib game and the cheating that was part of the game. The old man pegged out, clasped his hands over his head in a victory salute and laughed his gap-toothed laugh. "There, smarty, you didn't even see what I did! And I'm not gonna tell you, either! I won and I beat ya and I got one over on ya." The mute's silent laughter illuminated his face and once again Peter thought he could hear a faint echo of laughter, but before he could be sure, the old man rose and moved to switch on a battery-operated radio and the sound of music filled Peter's ears. He leaned back, and the sounds from the radio combined with the slow teasing progress of the second crib game lulled him to sleep. He didn't even open his eyes when the mute got up, moved to the couch, pulled Peter's legs onto the seat, took off the ugly black shoes and spread an old grey woollen blanket over the sleeping boy.

Small Peter was asking over and over again Why, why, why, but nobody could hear him ... he could see the bed that had been his for more than three months, and on it his clothes, neatly folded ... someone whose hands he thought he could recognize was lifting his clothes and putting them in a shopping bag, packing his life in a bag again, and then two bunks in a room, four boys, three besides himself, and he had to sleep in a bottom bunk knowing that just above his head was another bedspring, another mattress, another boy, a bigger boy who seemed okay but you never knew with bigger boys, and all of them fosters, not a real brother in the whole room, just fosters

He Who Would Sing looked over at the couch where the boy lay, his arms and legs moving feebly, his head twisting slowly from side to side. The mute rose suddenly, went to the couch, grabbed Peter roughly and moved him to the front door. So quickly that even the old man wasn't sure what was happening, He Who Would Sing had the door open and the boy's zipper down. Then he began to whistle softly.

Peter jerked awake. He wasn't in a room full of snakes and smoke, he was standing in the doorway and he could hear the sound of something dribbling in the yard. Standing beside Peter, grinning and urinating, was He Who Would Sing. Then Peter realized that he, too, was urinating.

"Well, now!" The old man sounded pleased. "Don't you learn something new all the time! I never knew until he told me just now that when he was a tad he used to pee the bed. Guess that's how he knew what was botherin' you."

It didn't make Peter feel any better to know someone else

used to have a problem. That's not much help when you've still got yours. But he was glad he hadn't peed the sofa; he wasn't sure what he'd have done if he'd wakened up and the couch had had a big wet stain on it.

He didn't know what he was supposed to do now, either. Sit on the chair or go back to the couch or what? Did they expect him to stay? He didn't want to do the wrong thing. "If you need another blanket, boy, just say so." The old man reached for the cards, beginning to shuffle them. "You don't have to freeze. Me, I like to sleep real warm, but him, the big bugger, he sleeps with nothin' on him but a sheet. I don't think that's natural. You watch a dog, now, he goes to sleep he puts his tail over his nose. A chicken, she tucks her head under her wing. A cat curls herself up in a ball and tucks her nose out of sight; only stands to reason if all the animals in nature try to cover theirselves up good and warm, it's natural to bundle up; but no talking to him sometimes, he's got a head like a rock when he wants. Strips hisself down, washes all over with cold water, dries hisself off and gets into bed in his bare pelt with nothin' on him but a sheet. Weird as hell, that guy."

Peter moved back to the couch, lay down and pulled the blanket over his shoulders. The old man's voice blended with the music from the radio, point and counterpoint, and Peter began to drift off, trying to listen.

"Before we got that pump in the house he'd go outside and stand under the stars scrubbin'. Could be snow fallin', he hadda have his night wash. Me, I wash in the morning. If animals hide their noses from night air, why take your whole body out in it?"

But Peter heard no more; he was sound asleep.

4

It was the smell and sound of frying ham that woke Peter up in the morning. The old man was washing his hands and face in a small round basin on the edge of the table, and He Who Would Sing was busy at the stove. Thick slices of ham sizzled in one large black frying pan and leftover mashed potato from supper the night before in another.

"Well, you woke up, did you," the old man smiled, gesturing an invitation to wash.

Peter hopped out of bed and went to the small basin, washing his hands and face in the same water the old man had used, drying himself on the same towel.

"Sleep good?" the old man asked, and Peter nodded. "Radio didn't keep you awake?" Peter shook his head, emptied the small basin and hung the towel behind the stove. He wiped off the table and began to set for breakfast.

"We sat up until real late playin' crib." The old man sipped his coffee, nodded his approval. "Musta been close to ten before we give up and went ta bed. Heard a thing on the radio, I guess it was the nine o'clock news we heard it on, huh?" The mute nodded agreement, turning the potatoes carefully. "We heard about this here boy . . . guess he's awful sick . . . seems like he took off from some kinda place, a hospital maybe . . ."

Peter backed for the door, his eyes welling with tears, his

mouth working, wanting to explain, knowing he could never explain.

"I guess this boy's been gone nearly a week and every police in BC must be out lookin' for him."

Peter whirled, headed out the door. He Who Would Sing started after him, but the old man called out sharply in Nootka, Leave him go, you can't keep a boy who don't want to stay, and even when the silent one slapped his hip and ran his fingers down a nonexistent yellow stripe on his pants, even then the old man would not give permission to chase the boy.

"Yes, they're looking for him," he agreed sadly, "and I know they'll catch him sure and maybe even lock him up again. But you can't make a caged bird sing and you can't tie up a boy like he was some kinda dog. He'll come back if it's Time for him to come back."

He Who Would Sing didn't agree with the old man and he showed it in his every move. He clattered the frying pans and slammed the coffee pot on the stove. He dumped the eggs into the pan with the ham and when he drank his coffee he blew into the cup and then slurped angrily. The old man tried hard to ignore the argument he was getting.

PETER RAN AWAY FROM THE CABIN, across the clearing, toward the bush. Why did they have to have a radio? They didn't have any electric lights, they didn't have a television and their stove was so old you had to put wood in it to get it to heat up, but they had to have a radio. No telephone, but they had a radio. And they knew he was being chased. They knew he was the boy who had run away.

He stopped running finally and sat down under a tree. He wished he'd had breakfast before they'd asked him about the radio. The smell of the cooking ham was still in his nostrils, the sound of the crackling fat still in his ears. It reminded him a bit of the sound that preceded the nightmares, the sound that preceded all the bad things that happened to him. The snake-thing had found him in the bush. It was the snake-thing that had chased him to the beach where he met the old man and the huge mute. If he left the bush the police would find him, if he stayed in the bush the snake-thing would find him.

They hadn't even really settled down to eat when he opened the door and walked back into the kitchen. The mute hurried to get the hopefully-stored breakfast out of the warming oven; he set the plate on the table and gestured at the waiting chair.

"You missed a good argument," the old man said placidly, hiding his surge of joy behind his carefully blank face. "This big fellow, he near banged the coffee pot through the top of the stove, just because I wouldn't let him chase you."

"I'm sorry," Peter whispered softly.

"Fella on the radio's always talkin' about that old man from Sweden who's in such good shape. He's always saying we all oughta get more exercise. Me, I don't see any sense atall in running for the good o' m'health; not on an empty stomach, anyway."

Peter knew the old man knew that wasn't why he'd been running, but he knew he didn't have to say so.

"Did you do like they say you did?" the old man asked, all sign of laughter gone from his face. "Did you set that fire in that school?"

"Yes, sir."

"Why!" The wrinkled raisin eyes demanded an answer.

"Things like that happen," Peter said slowly, feeling his throat tighten and his eyes well with tears. He knew before he even tried to explain, he knew nobody would believe him, he was just going to get into more trouble. But he had to answer. He Who Would Sing was demanding to know, his face speaking for him. "I was walking and the noises started and then I was in this place and everything was all burning . . . things like that happen, and I don't remember doing them. But I know when they say I did them they're telling the truth." He sniffed, hoping nobody would notice how close to crying he was.

"There's things," the old man spoke slowly, his eyes fixed on some point behind Peter's head, "there's spirit things that cause fires. They like to hang around where there's kids, that way nobody knows it's the spirits, they just blame the kids. Sometimes entire people just go poof and nothin' left but ashes, because of the spirit things."

Peter was crying now, and didn't care who saw him. The old man ignored the tears and just kept talking to that point on the wall behind Peter's head.

"I wouldn't want nothing like that to happen around here. So if any of them spirits show up and try to start a fire, don't stand around ditherin' and waitin' to get blamed." The slanted black eyes bored into Peter's own eyes. "You chuck a bucket'a water on the bugger!"

He could feel his head nodding, promising frantically to throw water, promising anything, anything as long as the blame didn't fall on him. Great racking sobs wrenched from his chest and he wanted to speak, but couldn't. The silent one whistled, stood up, pretended to unzip his fly and spray the room.

"He says if you can't get any water, just piss on it. But you put the bugger out!" And then the incredibly wrinkled old hand reached out, patted Peter's hand. "Now you eat up your food before it gets so old we have to give it to the gulls. And don't you feel shamed for crying, lotsa times I do it myself. Sometimes it's the only thing a person *can* do. You got any more'a that coffee, now that you're through chewin' my ear off and bein' mad at me?" He Who Would Sing reached for the coffee pot, grinning.

THE BOY WORKED AT THE WOODPILE, handling the axe with awkward inexperience. He Who Would Sing watched, waiting for the moment when the first flurry of energy had worn off and the boy would be willing to watch and see how to handle things properly. There was no use trying to show anyone the right way until they had found out for themselves how impossible it was to do it the wrong way. The boy had a good swing and enough sense to get his whole body into it, all he had to do was learn not to drive the axe head straight into the wood. He watched a flock of birds doing aerobatics in the sky, listened to the gradually slowing chop, chop, from the woodpile, and finally walked over and took the axe from the boy. He held the axe head above a block of wood, pointed straight down the way the boy had been doing it, and then shook his head slowly. He adjusted his grip so there was an almost imperceptible slant to the axe head, nodded, grinned, and handed the axe back. The boy stared at him with those strange green eyes, looked down at the axe, handed it back, wiggled his hands, and the mute understood and demonstrated the correct grip. Peter reached out and took the axe handle carefully, copying the grip almost exactly. The mute nodded, the boy shrugged, nodded, and turned back to the woodpile.

He Who Would Sing sauntered back to the steps, sat down and nodded.

"Think you're a regular schoolteacher, dontcha," the old man snickered happily. "You're worse'n an old grey cat that finally got her first kitten."

He Who Would Sing formed his fingers to resemble the beak of a duck and snapped quickly, yap yap yap.

"You think so, huh? I think he's a jump ahead of ya is what I think; that thing he did with his hands wasn't no accident, he knew before ya even went over what it was he was gonna ask and how he was gonna ask it."

Again the large fingers imitated a duck's quacking beak, yap yap yap, and silent laughter issued from the laughing mouth.

"What we gonna say to them police if they come around?"

He Who Would Sing stared at the old man, his face suddenly become vacuous, his eyes staring dully. He touched his throat, made pathetic moves with his mouth.

"Well, yeah, that's fine for you, do your Poor Loony thing, but what am I supposed to do?" And then the old man snorted to himself. "Well, I've lied about other things, I can lie about this."

The boy had sense enough to stop chopping and start stacking before the blisters formed on his hands, and when he had stacked all the freshly chopped wood, he joined them sitting on the steps, the sunlight warming their faces. After a few minutes he leaned over, tapped He Who Would Sing on the hand, touched himself on the chest and held out his own hands. The old man watched the silent one, the strong eye contact between the mute and the boy; then the huge hands moved slowly, the small hands copied carefully, and Peter had learned the sign for "Boy."

THEY WERE PLAYING CRIBBAGE AGAIN, each trying to cheat the other, and Peter was bored with nothing else to do but watch. He prowled the room, his eyes constantly returning to the dance cape, the sequined bird.

"You kinda like that old bugger, don't you," the old man grinned. "Him and me been together a long time. I got him when I was took into the society."

Peter's puzzlement grew as the old man went on talking. The mute watched, waiting.

"You ever seen a dance?" The old man rose, moved toward his dance cape, watching. Peter shook his head slowly. "You're what, eleven, twelve years old, and you've never seen a dance? Boy, your life ain't been much." He put the cape around his shoulders, fastened the throat-ties. "When I was your age I was studying." He looked down at the boy, face serious. "I'm a dancer. You know what it means to be a dancer?" Peter shook his head. "Well, it's a long hard study and one hell of an initiation. Special words to learn, special songs to sing. You eat only what they give you to eat, drink only what they give you to drink. Special exercises, special prayers, and then, when they think you're as ready as you're ever gonna be, there's tests; tests of your faith, your courage, and if you pass them, then there's the initiation." He gestured at the watching mute. "He knows. He hadda go through it, too. When you find your song, you're a member. You gotta find your own song, it's from inside you, and when you find it, everyone listens and they know who you are."

"How did he sing?" Peter asked softly.

"He sang. With his face and his hands and his legs and his eyes. And he cried. We heard him." The old man smiled. "We heard him good."

The lantern caught the design, the sequins glittered, the

bird moved around the room, carrying the old man with it, swooping and diving in time to the beat from the drum He Who Would Sing was playing. The old man held a carved cedar rattle in the shape of a strange bird, and the noise of the rattle blended with the soft beat of the drum and the strange sounds the old man was making, words in a language as old as the Island rocks. Peter sat on the sofa, his fingers softly tapping time on his knee, and he thought he had never seen anything so lovely. The music stopped, the old man stopped, the freewheeling bird became just a design on a blanket, and the old man sat down on a chair, breathing heavily.

THE ROOM WAS DARK, and Peter knew he had been asleep because just an eye-blink ago he had been watching the checkers game that had replaced the cribbage game, and the sound of the radio had toyed at the edges of his mind. Now the radio was quiet, the table cleared, and if there was a fire in the stove, it was a small and quiet fire, not even the sound of snapping wood could be heard. The carvings in the room seemed very different, strangely altered by shadows and the cool moonlight coming through the window. His eyes were drawn to the large carving on the wall, two animals coming out of a box. Strange animals, not fish, not . . . anything recognizable.

The strange sound was starting up again, a cricket-snap, a sound like the tink-a-click from the little toys in crackerjacks, sometimes a ladybug or a grasshopper, little metal things you held between your thumb and forefinger and squeezed together, tink-a-click, tink-a-click. A small firefly-light appeared in the corner near the stove, another seemed to float above the sofa, pinpointing his position. He knew he was sitting upright, back rigid, eyes staring, staring at the pinpoints of light that were gathering, forming a cone, inverting, spreading out, filling the room. He could hear his breathing harsh in his ears, feel his chest heaving, trying to scream, trying to yell for help, praying his legs would work so he could run

and suddenly the old man and the mute were standing in the middle of the room staring. Staring at Peter who was staring at them. They, too, were altered. This was not the feeble old man who yattered on garrulously, this old man had the same incredibly wrinkled face, the same gnarled hands and slanted raisin eyes, but

a carved stone amulet in the middle of his forehead, held in place by a soft leather thong that tied behind his head, another amulet at his throat, and on his head a woven bark headdress; from his shoulders the dance cape, feathers at wrist and ankle, something . . . secret . . . around his waist and in his hand the carved cedar rattle. Moving beside him the mute dressed in a blanket adorned with buttons, hundreds of little white buttons sewn in religious designs. Around the mute's throat a thong, and hanging from it a small bag.

"Give name to what you see," the old man intoned softly. "Give your fear a name, describe to me what you see."

"Nothing," Peter choked.

"Give name to what you see!" the old man's voice commanded. He knelt by the sofa, eyes boring holes in Peter's head. "I can keep it away from you for a little while, but not forever. Tell me what you see."

The mute knelt, his huge fingers tracing the pattern of the dancing lights, pointing out one of the firegleams, moving with it.

"He sees it too?" Peter gasped.

"Of course he sees it," the old man said calmly. "He sees it 'cause it's there. You can't see something that doesn't exist. If you see it, it's there and it's real. Give name to what you fear."

"I don't know the name," Peter said. "I see things, little lights dancing. And I hear things. Small clinking things, things like . . . like birds . . . or crickets . . . or small hard things hitting against each other, like . . ."

"Like the scales of a snake?"

Peter's eyes jerked to the strange design on the wall, the two animals coming from the box.

"Yes!"

"The lights and little noises are the Stlalacum. Stlalacum are strong medicine, strong magic. They are souls, souls of great men and women who have been priests, souls of great men and women who one day will be priests. They come to warn you. But that is all they can do, warn you; like me, they cannot keep the spirits away from you forever."

"I'm scared," Peter whispered.

"You got good reason to be scared, boy. But it's being scared got you into this mess; fear sends off waves and fear waves attract bad spirits just as sure as shit attracts flies. And you ain't been doing much to help yourself."

The Stlalacum lights were dancing wildly now, the chirping sound was louder, and in the corners of the room the vapours were forming, coming together, the snake-thing gathering strength, trying to reach past the power of the old man and the mute. Peter tried to run and the mute grabbed him, held him close.

"Don't run, boy!" the old man shouted. "You been running and running. You gotta learn to stand up for yourself, 'cause if you don't, that bugger's gonna get you. He's gonna get you and suck the soul outta you and you're gonna wind up worse than dead!"

Peter slumped suddenly, and He Who Would Sing drew his arm out from under the boy, stared meaningfully at his hand. Peter felt his face flame, knew the wet stain was spreading across the front of his jeans. "I'm always doing something bad," he confessed, feeling himself shrinking, shrinking to become the baby he really was, the baby who needed a diaper, who couldn't even find the toilet, who couldn't even make it to the front door to pee in the yard.

"You think you're bad?" The old man laughed suddenly, holding out his carved rattle. "See this? This here's Raven. Bad. Baddest bugger that ever lived, Raven is. Steals, swears, makes a mess all over everything. But he wasn't always that way. No sir, not even Raven was born bad."

The mute was busy taking off Peter's wet jeans, folding a dry towel underneath the boy so he didn't have to lie on a wet sofa, getting a dry blanket to spread over him, soothing him with touch and soft smile, nodding his head encouragingly. The old man settled himself into his story, giving his full attention to it.

"What it was, there was a lady wanted a baby. So what she did was, she prayed to Thunderbird; she'd get up first thing in the morning and go to a sacred place. Any time you've got something special to ask, you get there right at dawn when most people are still asleep and the ear of the creator isn't mucked up with yammering and asking, pleading and wanting. So the creator, he heard her and sent Thunderbird to help. Oh, she said, I have no baby and I want one so bad. And Thunderbird, finally he said Well, he said, I could give you a baby but it wouldn't be a Human baby, 'cause there's limits to what even Thunderbird can do. It'll be a god-person, he says, and god-persons aren't earth-persons and if you go from one reality to another there's changes have to happen. So, he says, if I give you this god-person baby, you see to it that it doesn't ever eat human food or something awful will happen. Well, that woman wanted a baby, and she promised, and Thunderbird he gave her this baby.

"Well, that was about the prettiest baby anybody ever saw. Big shiny eyes and a smile like fresh water on a hot day. Cuddled and cooed and give everybody wet kisses and everything was just wonderful for everybody.

"But then the baby started noticing things. Like people eating. He wasn't the least little bit hungry, but, being a baby, he was all for tryin' anythin' new. So the little bugger put himself to cryin' for food. Finally someone give him some. Well, that done'er! He turned total glutton, ate everything, buttons offa button blankets, dishes, pots, pans, you name'er, that kid ate'er. If they'da had radios he'da ate that, too.

"THAT DOES'ER, old Thunderbird roared, and he come down outta the sky with feathers flashing lightning and wings beating thunder and fog comin' outta his horns.

"Well, that mother she started cryin'. Don't blame me, I didn't do it, don't take my baby, I never give him no food, it was someone else done'er. Now Thunderbird has limits to what he can stand, and a mother cryin' for her baby, that's one of them. Okay, he says, I won't take him, but I gotta change him, can't have him like he is, he'll be eatin' dugout canoes and whaling gear next, then where'll we be. Changed him into a white bird. Now you keep him in a cage, he says, 'cause if he gets free, somethin' bad'll happen for sure.

"So things went fine, and she kept her white bird son in a cage and she was happy. Until that bird learned to talk. Lemme out, he'd say, lemme out and we'll go see grandma. Oh, momma, I love you, he'd say, lemme out and I'll give ya a big kiss. So the woman figures Well, if I close the doors and windows . . . and she did, and she let him out of the cage. Pretty little white bird that used to be a god-person went around that room in a flash. Ha ha ha, he said, fooled ya, he said, and he went *zip* up the smoke hole she'd forgot to close. Out the other end of it he came, covered with soot, no white left to him at all. Kaw kaw, he screeched, and sat in a tree, kaw kaw, fooled you. When they tried to catch him he crapped on their heads. Kaw kaw, no cage for me. Flew in and outta the windows stealing shiny things, eating everything he could get ahold of, screamin' insults . . . Well, there it is, old Thunderbird growled, now you see what happens when you don't listen . . . well, it's your problem now, I'm not doin' no more about this! And that's where we got ravens, stealing, swearing, shitting buggers who'll eat anything, even buttons and clams shells. But he wasn't born bad, boy. Nothing and nobody is."

Peter wanted to smile, he wanted to speak, but his eyes were closing and the blanket was so warm, the soft stroking on his arm so gentle . . .

The old man looked down at him, the smile wiped from his face. "We got us a buncha trouble," he said softly, and then he felt his eyes drawn to the double-headed carving on the wall. Sisiutl, the double-headed sea serpent. "We got us a whole big buncha trouble."

IN THE MORNING PETER'S INSTITUTION JEANS WERE STILL WET. The mute had washed them and hung them on the oven door to dry but the waist and the thick material at the pockets were still wet. They found an old pair of jeans that belonged to the wizened old man and they cut off the legs, unevenly, and pulled them tight around Peter's waist with a length of cord.

"You ain't gonna win no prize for best-dressed man, but then we ain't givin' no prizes today," the old man decided. He Who Would Sing grabbed a piece of kindling wood, held it like a cane, postured and tipped an imaginary hat. Peter took the kindling stick and strolled across the kitchen the way he had seen an actor do in a movie once, an actor being a duke or a prince. The trousers flapped around his legs, the ugly romeo shoes looked huge and comical on his feet, the boy pranced and paraded, and for a minute he almost felt like a noble, or like an actor busy being a noble.

When being a noble paled, they had breakfast, did the work that needed doing, and then they went for a walk, Peter holding the old man's hand, not feeling at all ashamed of holding hands the way little kids did. They crossed the clearing and walked through the bush, Peter's eyes busy, looking everywhere for the smoke-threat, the slithery scare-thing.

And then they were by the seashore again. Not the cove where he found the oysters and the old man, not the same place at all. A stretch of sand, long, waist-high yellow grass, and a host of long-legged birds running on the damp sand, poking busily with their beaks, running with awkward stilt-steps, piping to each other.

Peter's eyes were drawn to the large black rocks that guarded the shore, rocks twisted and scored by the action of the waves, rocks that seemed to reach upward, pleading . . .

And the trees at the spit, totally barkless, bleached white as bones, corkscrewing from the ground upward, the very grain of the wood spiralling, not just gnarled branches or wind-warped shapes, but a steadily rising spiral of wood, dead fingers pointing to the heavens.

"Them's what Sisiutl done," the old man said quietly,

sitting on a sunwarmed log. The mute sprawled on the sand, his fingers drawing designs, his face calm. "The Sisiutl is a sea monster, one of the terrors from the kingdom of the sea. He's got a head at either end of his body so he can see where he's been as well as where he's going. When he comes up out of the water, the tides rise higher than they ever do; when he breathes the fog rolls in and you can't see where you're going. If he swishes himself, boats are thrown around like they were little bitty sticks, and when he swings himself in a rage, the water boils in whirlpools and anybody that gets sucked in doesn't ever get found again. Because he's a water creature, he can live anywhere there's water: rivers, creeks, streams, the dew on grass—he can even fall with the rain and ride on the damp fog. He can change his shape, because he's magic; he can be fog himself, or he can be what he really is, the biggest, shiniest, most powerful snake-fish that ever lived."

Something inside Peter was trembling, his stomach was becoming a knot, he could feel the muscles in his legs tightening, preparing to run again. The mute touched him, patted the sand beside him, and Peter sank gratefully beside the powerful man with the soft brown eyes.

"He's so scary that only a fool wouldn't feel it. His eyes flash ice fire and his tongue spits horror. He lives off the souls he steals from the Living Dead. Sisiutl, he smells fear and it makes him hungry, and he sets out after the people; he can chase'em anywhere there's water. And because our bodies are mostly water, he can always find what he needs. Jails is fulla people like that, the ones who walk and talk and even eat and sleep but don't know how to Live, can't Live, because Sisiutl has their soul.

"What you have to do is stare him down. Just face him, that's all. First you find something to believe in, something you Know isn't ever going to let you down, and then, when Sisiutl comes after you, you just hang onto what you Know, and you stare back at him. Because if you try to run, he's gonna start blowing with both mouths at the same time, and you'll start spinning, spinning, spinning until your soul busts loose and flies out through the top'a your head. You'll spin away from your body and people will hear your voice in the screamin' wind of first autumn, and you're Living Dead and nobody can never do nothing for you.

"Them trees ... they tried to run, and Sisiutl blew them and they spun until the bark popped off and only the roots kept them from flying up in the sky. Them rocks ... same thing ... they saw him and didn't have any faith and got all twisted and wrenched, and only because they're the tops'a mountains they didn't take off in the wind from them two ugly mouths.

"When he comes, if you know any protecting words, you say them. If you know any good spirit songs, you sing them. If you've got a charm or a magic to hang onto, you hang onto it. But you stand your ground, and you just stare back at him, even if you're so scared you can't make your bowels behave.

"'Cause he's gonna have to come close to get you! And he'll come close enough that you'll smell the ugly stink comin' from them two mouths. And them four eyes are gonna drill holes in you ..."

Peter was almost hypnotized, his eyes wide, his mouth half open, his skin pale.

"... closer'n'closer he's gonna come, aiming for your

mouth, so he can suck out your breath. Closer'n'closer until . . . he's gotta turn both'a his heads toward you . . . and when he does . . . left head is gonna see right head . . . right head is gonna see left head . . .

"Who sees the other half of self, sees Truth.

"And that's all old Sisiutl has ever really wanted. He don't want souls, he only takes'em cause he thinks they'll have some Truth for him . . . he don't realize the only souls he gets are the ones that don't have a Truth to hang onto. And so you just stand there, and he sees the other halfa hisself, and he's found Truth.

"And he'll bless you with his magic, and your Truth will be yours forever. Lotsa times the poor bugger'll come back, to get another glimpse of your Truth, and each time he'll be just as scary as he ever was, but he won't be able to hurt you because he'll have blessed you with his magic. He'll just come, and you'll just stand and stare back, and he'll see his face and he'll go.

"And the Stlalacum will come to see you, reminding you that all the Truth you ever need is right in back of your own two eyes."

Peter stared into the slanted black eyes of the incredibly old man, and felt himself being pulled into something . . . Something . . .

"And you'll never be Alone again, boy."

THE OLD MAN WAS DOZING IN THE SUN, the mute was prowling the beach looking for good carving wood, and Peter was following a bird, hoping it would lead him back to its nest. Pretending not to be looking at the bird, he moved carefully away from the beach toward the thicket where he had noticed the bird coming and going busily.

He had to get down on his hands and knees and crawl into the thicket, slowly pushing aside the stalks and branches. Ahead of him he could see the bird's nest, even see a hint of a small brown-speckled egg

and then it was coming at him, sliding noiselessly through the thicket, the slimy snake shape, heading straight for him, heading for his mouth, his throat, the stink of it filling his nostrils, choking him. He tried to back out of the thicket, not caring if his flailing arms were scaring the birds, not caring that he was turning the thicket into a shaking mass of stalks and budding leaves. The thicket, angry at such rough treatment, hooked his clothes, scratched his legs, and then the cold and ugly stink-fog was wrapping around his throat, filling his nose and mouth, cutting off his wind, cutting off his breath, smothering his whimpered cry for help, and the Stlalacum he had thought were birdsong were dancing insanely, unable to help, unable to interfere.

The old man jerked awake, his ears ringing with the Stlalacum warning, his inner eye registering the struggle he could not see.

"Ka-coots!" he yelled. "Ta-naz!" and the mute spun around, his keen eyes registering immediately the wildly flailing thicket, the boy's legs protruding and kicking. He ran, stumbling in his eagerness, reached out, grabbed the desperately thrashing legs, and mindless of briars or thorns, jerked the boy from the thicket.

Peter's eyes were rolled back, his tongue protruding and already turning blue, his fingers were gouging deeply into his throat, his chest heaving frantically. He Who Would Sing drew back his massive fist, concentrated all his attention on one point on the boy's jaw, and then punched, a short, sharp, powerful punch. Peter went limp, his arms dropping to his sides.

WHEN HE AWOKE IT WAS DARK OUTSIDE and the lantern in the cabin was lit. Shadows danced on the wall and a happy snapping sound came from the wood stove. The mute was sitting on the floor beside the sofa, sitting, waiting, waiting.

"My face is sore." Peter heard the locked-in tears in his own voice. His head pounded and his stomach muscles were tender. He could barely focus his eyes; he felt as if all he wanted to do was roll over and go to sleep.

He Who Would Sing nodded, tried to smile, then reached out and helped Peter from the sofa. Together they walked to the door, opened it, went out into the night and walked to the small, cedar-shake outhouse. Peter went in alone, and when he came back out He Who Would Sing was waiting for him. They walked back to the cabin together.

"I been doing magic," the old man announced soberly, his eyes staring at Peter from under the cedar-bark headdress, the shaman stones firmly laced in place. "I can keep that bugger away for a little while, but not forever. You gotta learn some Truth, boy, you gotta find some Faith, because I'm an old man and magic ain't easy at the besta times."

Peter felt himself trembling, his head was pounding and his eyes didn't want to focus on anything except the carving on the wall, the threatening cedar carving of Sisiutl the double-headed sea serpent.

"I can't do anything if you don't help me," the old man intoned as the mute put the boy back to bed and covered him with the blanket. "If you want, I'll get you Grabbed, but you gotta be ready to do anything I tell you, no matter how silly it seems."

Peter's head wouldn't even nod when he wanted it to, his hands wouldn't lift off the sofa, all he could do was stare deeply into the eyes of He Who Would Sing, stare until he felt himself sliding out of his own head, being drawn deep, deep into the soft brown eyes.

The mute spent the night sleeping on the floor beside the sofa. Guarding the boy.

5

THE HANDLE OF THE SHOVEL WAS TOO LONG FOR HIM, he didn't know how to hold it properly, but the way the blade bit into the earth was satisfying, and when he had struggled and lifted a clod of earth, the smell made him feel good inside. He sent the sharp silvery shovel blade into the clod, breaking it into smaller and smaller pieces, helping He Who Would Sing prepare the garden plot.

"Wish I could remember if you plant root vegetables at the full of the moon or the skinny of it," the old man muttered, sitting on the steps, planning each row, each seed. "Some things go in one time, other things go in another time. Rows oughtta face north and south, I remember that. Time was I could remember everything, certain and clear as a bell. Must be getting old," he decided, shaking his head.

The sun was almost hot; Peter's shirt was stained with sweat and the scratches on his legs stung with the salt. He could feel his hair sticking to his damp forehead. He put the blade against the earth, jumped up and landed with his feet on the metal lips, balancing carefully. He Who Would Sing reached out and pushed and Peter and the shovel fell sideways. He landed in the soft earth, hearing inside his head the happy sound of laughter from the mute throat.

They worked all morning and part of the afternoon and

when the garden plot was shovelled, hoed, raked and ready, they put the tools in the old shed and left the waiting fertile earth to the sun and wind. The old man said the earth was like a woman, you got her ready and you waited for her to let you know. When she'd felt the sun and wind and seen the moon and stars she would welcome the seeds.

"Don't never try to rush her," he lectured gently. "Not the earth and not a woman. Nor a man, neither, for that matter. You just do what you gotta do to help it get ready, and have some patience."

He Who Would Sing packed a lunch and they set out from the cabin, walking through the green woods. Once or twice Peter reached up to touch the bag of magic the mute had given him, the same bag that had swung from the neck of the silent one. It was reassuring to know that even if Sisiutl was lurking in the bush, he couldn't come close to Peter because of the magic bag and the power of his two friends.

The water was cold, but it felt good; the sweat and dust sluiced from his body, his skin turned pink, and he felt himself responding to the call of his own body, kicking and splashing the water, sending droplets to glisten in the sunlight. His clothes, neatly folded, lay on a rock on shore, and all the skin on his body was bathed in clean river water. He Who Would Sing stripped off his clothes and walked into the river, swimming with powerful strokes for the other side. Peter tried to swim alongside, kicking furiously, and the silent one slowed his stroke, and then suddenly dove under the water and came up on the other side, spitting a stream of clear water at Peter.

The old man sat on the bank with his feet trailing in the cool water and his laughter rang over the river, lost itself in the green trees on the bank. The mute grabbed Peter, lifted him high over his head, then threw him into the water. The boy's yelp of surprise was cut short as his head went under water and when he came back up again he splashed a spray at He Who Would Sing. He climbed on the mute's shoulders and dove into the river; they filled their lungs with air, dove down and swam between each other's legs—one standing, spraddlelegged, the other duckdiving, coming up, and standing spraddlelegged for the other one to swim. They found a length of rope and hung a swing from the branch of a tree and the old man chortled as Peter cut loose with a Tarzan yell, swung out over the water, let go of the rope and landed with a splash in the river. When He Who Would Sing swung out on the rope his mouth was open but only the inner ear could hear his yodel.

"Do it again," Peter urged, and the burly man nodded, reached for the rope and swung out over the river. "Yaaaay!" Peter screamed, "I'm makin' noise *for* ya! Hooooo!" And when He Who Would Sing let go of the rope, the boy's surrogate yodel crashed against the old man's ears and then turned into his own laughter. The mute came from the river, his powerful muscles rippling, his face wreathed in a satisfied smile. He dried himself on the towel, pulled his pants on and sat down, reaching for the picnic bag.

"Hey, boy, if you don't get over here it'll all be gone," the old man invited.

Thick sandwiches and a thermos of coffee, homemade cookies and fruit, they ate until even the boy could eat no more. "This is the nicest place I ever saw in my life," he said suddenly. "I think I'm going to call it my special place. My place,"

"We was here first," the old man teased.

"Fight you for it," the boy invited, pretending to throw a punch.

The old man's hand darted out and he grabbed the boy's wrist, wrestled him onto his back and started tickling him. The boy didn't laugh, didn't struggle, the tickling didn't bother him. He reached out with his free hand and pinched the old man's nose. Gently.

"I've got you and I'm not gonna let go," he said quietly. Their eyes locked. The old man stopped tickling. "You win," he said. "You've got me sure enough."

He Who Would Sing reached for an apple and bit into it with a satisfying crunch, chewing slowly.

"We used to come here a lot," the old man mused, "when he was young . . . and that's a bit of time past, too! There were lotsa kids here, then. But the town grew out the other way and the people went where there was work in town, and I guess most everybody forgot about this place. Almost forgot about it myself. Lotsa things I almost forgot about." And suddenly his tone changed. "By god, boy, them pants are a mess. We gotta get you a decent pair of pants; them's disgustin'." He turned to the mute. "We got any money?"

The mute laughed silently, shook his head.

"Well, no matter, we got us them carvings. Just have to go see that pinchfaced fella in the tourist store is all."

But when it was time to go home the old man could not get up off the riverbank. He Who Would Sing had gathered up the picnic leftovers and repacked them in the bag, then had walked on ahead, expecting the old man and the boy to follow; the old man tried to rise and couldn't.

"Well, now," he said, his face paling with shock, "well, now, that's somethin'."

"Singer!" the boy shouted. "Singer, come back!" The powerful body turned. He Who Would Sing came back, moving quickly. He knelt, reaching out and touching the old man's legs, his eyes searching the worried old face.

"Don't feel a thing, son," the old man confessed. "Not even your fingers."

The mute's hands flashed, Does it hurt?

"Don't hurt. I feel a bit funny; I think I'm scared is all. Didn't get dizzy or sick feeling, they just won't move."

He Who Would Sing lifted the old man easily, strode off through the gathering darkness, and Peter followed, feeling forgotten and alone. He stopped once, briefly, to gather up the picnic bag the mute had dropped, then scurried after his friends.

They put the old man to bed and Peter fussed over him, plumping the pillow, getting the dance cape and putting it over his shoulders to keep him warm and protect him from the bad luck. He Who Would Sing mixed dried herbs and powders from the store of medicine prepared from plants he collected himself, and he gave the brew to the old man to drink.

"Couldn't make it taste good, I suppose," the old man muttered.

"If it tastes rotten it's because it's good for you," Peter reminded him.

"Shoulda been a mother, that guy."

"Men can't be mothers! Only ladies can be mothers."

"Shows what you know," the old man sighed, relaxing as he felt the herbal tea taking effect. "Anybody can be a mother. One time Copper Woman had to go away for a long time to do some magic, and she left her nearly new baby with her oldest boy." He sipped the herb tea, talking softly, with many pauses. "She was gone an awful long time, but when she came back the cabin was clean and tidy, the baby had grown and was fat and learning to walk. There was dried fish and smoked meat and a big store of oolichan oil. Even a new dress to welcome her home, made all fancy with little shells and beads. Her oldest boy, he done all that himself."

"Yeah, but he wasn't a Mother," Peter insisted. "He was just babysitting. He didn't have that baby."

"You figure just having a baby makes someone a mother? What about Raven's mother? She didn't *have* that baby, it was give to her. What about people that adopt babies? Or is the mother the one that gives it away?"

"Only ladies can be mothers." Peter felt threatened and knew his face was closing up, knew the lids were coming down over his eyes. He knew the old man could see this, and he wished he could stop what was happening to his face.

The old man gestured to where the mute was carving at the kitchen table, papers spread on the floor to catch the shavings. "Want to give it a try? Be something to do. Something more interesting than listening to an old man's yammer."

"I don't know how."

"So he'll show ya. You could learn."

"No, I couldn't. I can't learn anything. They say I've got a . . . a learning disability . . . it's got a real long name and it means I can't learn anything at all. I can't even read," he admitted.

"Izzat so? I don't read myself. He does, the big fella. He reads lots." He handed the cup to the boy and settled back against his pillows, relaxing with the herbs and with relief at the way the closed-in look had faded from the boy's face. For a minute or two there he hadn't even recognized Peter, had been able to see only a threatened and potentially violent stranger. "In the old days, we done things a lot different. In the old days kids weren't expected to Know anything, they were just kids.

They did their kid things and lived their kid lives and watched people doing what needed to be done. After a while of watching, well, maybe the kid would want to try it, and so he'd go to whoever was best at what it was he wanted to try, and that person would show him how it was done. Then the kid would give it a try. Didn't matter if it didn't turn out right; he wasn't supposed to *do*'er, you see, he was only giving it a try." His old eyes seemed fixed on some point in time totally unknown to Peter or even to He Who Would Sing, who listened intently, carving slowly. "And anything we had to say that was important, why we'd put it into a story and find four different ways to tell that story. Four, she's a magic number, she's complete. Tell a fella something four times and he's never going to forget. You tell him a story about something one way, and then you change'er around and tell him the same story, but a different way, and when he's heard it four times, he knows."

"Wouldn't do any good," Peter said sadly. "I'm really stupid. They tried everything. Even remedial class. It wouldn't work with me."

"What wouldn't?"

"Tell me something four times or four hundred times, it wouldn't do any good."

"Why would anybody do that?" The old man's brow furrowed; he seemed to have forgotten his train of thought.

"You said," Peter insisted, his face flaring with anger, "you said if you tell a fella something four times he won't ever forget! And I say I can't learn," he almost snarled.

"Izzat so?" The old man grinned suddenly. "You learned about four, didn't you?"

THE OLD MAN WAS ASLEEP, the soft music from the radio filled the room and Peter sat hunched over his cards, trying to count his hand. A nine and a six made fifteen for two, but could you use that same six with a seven and a two for another two points? He looked up in time to see the big tanned hand sneak towards the pegboard.

"You move without you're supposed to and I'm gonna fix you," Peter whispered softly.

He Who Would Sing shrugged, grinned, and pulled his hand away from the crib board.

"Just because I'm not very big, that doesn't mean I'm not someone to watch out for—oh no, don't you fool yourself." His voice droned on in unconscious imitation of the sleeping old man. "You might think all those muscles of yours have got me scared, but that's not right. I'm not scared of you."

IN THE MORNING the old man had to be carried out to the out-house in the back yard, then he had to be carried back to sit by the kitchen table to wash himself in the basin of warm water Peter brought him.

"Foolish way to end your life," he muttered to himself. "Being lugged around like when you were a baby. Brings it all full circle, just like they said."

But he ate his breakfast with good appetite and when the dishes were done and the cabin tidy, He Who Would Sing carried him out to sit in the sun and supervise the planting of the garden.

"You be gentle now," he cautioned. "You walk soft and do things easy, like it's supposed to be."

The rows ran north and south the way they were sup-posed to, and the lines were straight. The powerful mute and the stocky little boy planted carefully: three corn seeds and a pumpkin seed in one hillock, three corn seeds and a squash seed in the next hillock. Three corn seeds and a vegetable marrow seed in another hillock, then four corn seeds to finish the cycle and bring it complete. They smiled at each other often, and the perfume from the waiting earth was like nothing Peter had ever smelled before: it made him sleepy and excited all at the same time. He touched the strong forearm of the mute, then tapped his own nose, pointed at the earth and smiled. The mute nodded and closed his eyes, a dreamy expression coming over his face; then he grinned and pretended to pop his thumb in his mouth. Peter frowned and the mute tapped his chest, repeated his thumbsucking motion and pretended to snuggle something ... someone ... Peter shook his head slowly, he couldn't remember being cuddled against a warm breast, he couldn't remember Her ever wanting to ...

"Just leave me alone," he screamed suddenly. "Just leave me alone about that. I don't know what you're talking about so just shut up!"

"Oh, don't be so damned miserable," the old man said sharply. "Just because you don't know about it yourself don't mean it isn't there!"

"He's always talking about stuff like that! He's always talking to me about all kinds of things I don't know anything about!"

He marched away from the obviously laughing mute; already he was feeling more than a little bit foolish. He sat on the wood-chopping block and glared, but nobody seemed to care that he was glaring. The old man sat in the sun and the mute went back to planting the seeds and after a half hour of sulking and feeling sorry for himself, Peter moved back to the garden and worked alongside He Who Would Sing.

A FEW DAYS LATER, when it was obvious the old man was going

to need to be carried for quite some time, maybe even forever, they set off to town, the old man insisting he had said they'd get proper pants for Peter and by golly they would. The institution jeans were getting too tight for him, but they were better than the make-shift cut-offs, so he wore them, even though he worried that someone might recognize them and know he was one of Those Boys from That Place. His shirt was ripped, but the old man darned the rip so it almost didn't show, and maybe wouldn't have shown at all if they'd been able to match the colour of the thread to the colour of the shirt.

They walked through the bush to the roadway, He Who Would Sing carrying the old man easily, and when they got to the roadway they sat down and waited for a car to come. The first two or three that came didn't stop, but finally a man in a battered pickup truck pulled alongside them and stopped.

"Where you heading?" he asked casually.

"Campbell River," Peter answered, jumping into the pickup box and helping the old man over the side of the truck. The driver looked curious. "He hurt his leg," Peter explained, "so we have to help him a bit."

"Hope it gets better soon." The driver didn't seem very interested, and when He Who Would Sing had vaulted into the pickup box, the driver put the truck in gear and drove off down the highway. The three in the back grinned at each other and settled back to watch the scenery slip past, their hair blowing in the wind.

Peter carried the cardboard box of carvings and He Who Would Sing carried the old man. Some of the townspeople turned to stare; a crippled old Indian, a mute of indeterminate heritage, and a young boy with a wild shag of hair sun-bleaching to a dark blond.

Peter snooped around in the tourist store while the old man did the talking.

"Well, boys," the store manager hedged, "I don't know, it's been kinda slow so far, not many tourists yet. Business is kind of slack . . ."

"Well, tell us the best you can do," the old man grinned, "and if it isn't good enough, well, maybe the fellow down the street can do better . . ."

In the end they got more than enough for what they needed. The carvings were good and the store manager knew they would sell quickly; he placed an order for more and tried to get the old man to promise him an exclusive option on anything they carved. The old man said he'd be sure to think of this place first, but he wouldn't be committed to an exclusive anything.

They bought new blue jeans and a plaid shirt, a blue jean jacket that was a size too big (room to grow, the old man said) and then they went to the shoe store and got a pair of running shoes. Peter was glad to put the ugly black institution shoes in a bag; his feet in the new runners looked as if they belonged to him again. They went to the fish and chip shop for supper and all of them agreed that it was a fine meal, a very fine meal. After they had eaten all they could hold, they walked up and down the main street staring at all the things in the store windows, not caring that people were staring at them. Then they went to a movie and cheered when the cavalry cleaned up on the Indians again.

They got a ride home in another pickup, this one half filled with sacks of grain, and it was all Peter could do not to fall asleep leaning against the sacks.

6

PETER STOOD IN THE MIDDLE OF THE ROOM wearing only his undershorts, and the magic bag the mute had given him to hang around his neck. The old man and He Who Would Sing sat on the sofa, watching him with expressionless faces, their eyes sombre, their dance capes glittering in the light.

"Raven," Peter said carefully, "is the trickster. His voice is a sharp stone that cuts the day. He tricks and is tricked, does jokes that often turn on him. Raven is the one who never uses force. He uses his wits, and his magic, but never force. Once, a long time ago, on an island far to the north, there lived an old fisherman and his daughter who had a round, bright, shiny thing they kept hidden in a carved cedar box, a round bright shiny thing they called . . . moon." He moved slowly, his feet tracing the pattern the mute had shown him, his hands and arms beginning to tell the story as the two shamans had demonstrated. "Raven loves bright shiny things. Raven wanted the moon. So he used his wits, and his magic, and he flew through the night to the fisherman's house, and with magic he turned himself into a baby girl, lay down on the doorstep and began to cry." Peter lay down on the floor, miming the actions of the raven. "Wah, wah, wah."

"The sound of the crying wakened the fisherman and his daughter; they opened the door and found the little baby girl crying in the night. The daughter wanted the baby but the fisherman wasn't happy about it, so they had a long talk. But in the end the daughter won and she took the baby into the house. The fisherman went to sleep and the daughter played with the baby, but after a few minutes the baby began to whimper. What's she snivelling about, the fisherman wanted to know. She wants to play with the b-o-x, the daughter answered. Well she can't play with the b-o-x. I told her that, said the daughter, that's why she's snivelling. Oh, the fisherman snarled, let her play with it, what harm can she do? And so the raven-baby got to play with the carved box. She used the same crying trick to get the daughter to open the box, and she used it again to get the daughter to give her permission to pat the moon and touch the moon, to lift the moon from the box and play with it. She cooed and gurgled softly, playing with the moon carefully, and the daughter was fooled and went to sleep. Then Raven turned himself back into a bird and he tucked the moon under his chin, but just as he was about to fly up the smokehole, the laughter in his throat bubbled out . . . kaw! . . . and the fisherman and his daughter woke up. They chased him and nearly caught him, but in the end he went up the smokehole. He flew and he flew until his wings began to grow weary. And presently the moon became too heavy to hold under his chin, so he flew to the top of the highest mountain, and then he threw the moon up in the sky where it caught on the corner of a cloud and it's there to this day. And that," Peter concluded carefully, "is how the moon got in the sky."

He waited until the old man nodded permission to leave and then he went to get a glass of water for his dry throat. He Who Would Sing came over and patted his shoulder, nodding approval, and Peter was glad he had spent the hours he had practising and memorizing.

"You done okay," the old man grinned. "You told that one real good, and when you were being Raven you moved just like a bird; except next time, you got to do more of a hop, ravens are perky fellas, they kinda skip along when they're walking."

A few days later the old man and the mute walked him through the woods to a cluster of small, unpainted houses. The old man, totally unselfconscious about his infirmity, rode piggy-back, the mute seeming not to even notice the slight weight. They went into a house where several old men sat waiting, and Peter had to repeat the raven story for the old men who stared at him, stared through him, and when he had finished they spoke to the old man in a strange language. And then the mute lifted the old man and they left for home.

Peter wanted to ask questions, he wanted to know who the old men were, what part they were playing in his life, but he knew not to ask any questions, to simply learn to do what the old man said was necessary.

He learned to tell a good piece of wood from a piece that would split when only half carved. He learned how to coax the birds to the feeding station and he learned how to clean and fillet rock cod.

THEY CARRIED THE OLD MAN TO THE ROAD in the early morning and got a ride into town with the mail truck. The man in the tourist store was glad to see them, and they got a better price for their work than they had the previous time. The big sun-god carving the mute had been working on brought almost as much as all the other things together, and that gave them more than enough money for what they needed.

The junk store was crowded and dusty, things were piled haphazardly all over the place, and Peter wandered, fascinated, through the treasure trove. Skates and frisbees, old clothes and pictures that at one time had meant something to somebody. And standing in the back, half hidden under a pile of old magazines, the wheelchair.

The spokes were a bit bent in places and the seat was frayed, it needed a lot of cleaning up, oiling and adjusting, but, battered as it was, the old man sat in it proudly, and Peter practically strutted down the street, pushing his friend, helping to be the legs, the strength. He Who Would Sing was quite content to let Peter push, knowing that sooner or later the boy would get tired and his own strength would be needed. They pushed, rode and walked their way past the store windows, through the people who this time barely glanced at them. They bought big ice cream cones and enjoyed the cool richness. And they bought groceries and piled the bags on the seat with the old man, pushing everything in the squeaky old wheelchair.

They didn't have to thumb a ride home, they just started pushing the wheelchair down the highway and some people in a maxivan stopped and offered them a lift.

That night the old man sat at the kitchen table stringing beads on a loom, beads he had bought in town, a loom the mute had fashioned for him. Peter practised his drumming and chanting, the mute showed him again the proper steps, and the old man pored over his work. Peter supposed he had found a new way to make money from the tourist store.

The next day the old man decided not to go fishing with them; he stayed home, working on the beads. When they came home with half a dozen good-sized rainbow trout, the old man was still sitting in his wheelchair, stringing beads and muttering to himself. They cooked the fish for supper and he took time from his beading to eat with them, but as soon as the meal was finished, even before Peter had the table cleared, the old man was back at his self-appointed task.

"No wonder the white man took over this country," he muttered aloud. "First he give us beads and we went nearsighted trying to use'em ... then he come in and snuck everything away from us. Damn clever people, the white man."

Peter finished the dishes, cleaned the stove and wiped the countertop, then moved to sit at the table, watching. After a while the mute placed a small loom in front of Peter. Peter stared at it, his lips working slightly, then he stared at the old man's hands then down at the loom, and finally, after many minutes, he began to string beads and weave them on the loom, using his tongue as much as his fingers or eyes, working clumsily and slowly.

"That's got'er." The old man sighed with satisfaction. Then he beckoned to Peter to come stand beside him, and he fastened the beaded belt around Peter's waist. "Need somethin' to hold up them pants," he grinned.

Peter's eyes widened; he unbuckled the belt, stared. "Nobody ever gave me anything like this before ..."

"Nobody ever gave me a noisy boy before," the old man replied, softly. "Here, lemme show you." He laid the belt on the table, pointing to the beaded designs. "Four kingdoms make creation complete: the kingdom of the sea ... the killer whale; the kingdom of the air ... the eagle; the underground kingdom ... the magic earth creature—see his big paws, for diggin'; and this kingdom, with bear the brother of mankind."

Peter stared at the central, dominant design on the belt, a box with a face on it and a head coming from either end of the box. "What's this?" he asked softly.

"Mythical sea monster," the old man answered, his eyes fixed on the Sisiutl carving on the wall. "He's miles long, his breath is fog and when he surfaces, the waves go real high on the beach . . ."

"The Sisiutl?" Peter was trembling, barely able to hold his belt, staring in shock at the old man. "But . . ."

"He's in a spirit box, boy," the old man said, very calmly. "A spirit box can protect you. Anytime you're bothered, you just do magic and catch the spirit, put him in a box, and then he has to work for you, not against you. A spirit box is so strong even the design of one can protect your back. 'Course that still leaves your front. You're supposed to look after that yourself."

"It won't work," Peter blurted. He could hear the harsh clacking sounds; already the small lights were dancing, seeming to be centred around the carving on the wall. "Look, he's getting mad! He doesn't want to be locked in a box!"

"Just do your magic, son. Just say your words and—"

"It won't work. It's just stories. Little kid stories!"

"Spirits aren't fairy tales." The old man managed to stand up, hanging onto the edge of the table, his knuckles white, his face stern, and for the first time his voice trembled with anger. "You have some respect, boy!"

"Bullshit!" Peter raged, feeling his face closing in, feeling the shutters coming down over his eyes. "Bull . . . shit! Bullshit bullshit bullshit!"

The mute made a move to restrain him. Peter whirled, eyes blazing, face contorted. "Just keep your hands to yourself, you big Loony. Crazy man! Bothaya! Crazier'n hell. Even crazier'n mol Go to hell. Bothla you! LOONY!" And he raced for the door, running right through the host of dancing Stlalacum lights, heading into the night. The old man made a desperate lunge for Peter, his withered legs gave out, and he fell to the floor. He Who Would Sing moved to help the old man, hearing the sound of the door slamming shut.

HE HAD SEEN SOMETHING LIKE THIS BEFORE. He had sat in a darkened movie house and watched the princess, maybe it was Snow White, running through the forest, and all the trees turning into Scaries and grabbing for her. He had seen it all before, but this was worse. That other was just a movie, you could sit in the padded chair and hold your popcorn box and remind yourself it was all just lights and shadows and actors and film. This was real. The trees towered over him, blocking out any hint of moonlight or starlight, the branches slapped him, the vines and salal bushes grabbed his feet. Stlalacum danced wildly, the sound of their chirping setting his teeth on edge, and the disembodied voices of his dreams were merged with the legends he had learned . . . *Haw Haw Haw, Raven . . . Nothing but trouble since the day you were born . . . Bad Boy Nothing But Trouble Kaw Haw Kaw Lemme out we'll go for a walk . . .* Tree branches became policeman's hands and the sound of the slithering in the tree tops grew louder, louder, as the thing came closer, closer . . .

He fell to the ground, almost babbling with terror. His eyes strained in the darkness, his heart thudded against his rib cage

and there it was, right in front of him, coming closer, closer. He rose to his feet, his back pressed against the bole of a tree. There was no place left to run to, the forest was aiding the Sisiutl.

He was longer than anything Peter had ever seen, even longer than a train; taller than anything, longer and taller and every inch of him, every scale on his body, glittered, pulsed and exuded a smell that sometimes reminded Peter of boiled cabbage, sometimes of hardboiled egg yolk, sometimes of the nose-biting smell of a freshly struck wooden match. Silver scales and red ones, black ones and bright yellow bands, like a huge red-racer snake, and the strange dogfishgreen eyes glaring, glaring, the teeth snarling, the pulp-mill stink fog-breath coming from both mouths and a sound from him like when you shove a stick deep in the mud and then yard it back out again, sshllluuup!

Peter wanted to scream but his throat was sealed so tight he could barely breathe; he wanted to run but his legs wouldn't move.

Sshhllluuuppp, it moved closer, the silver-shine scales clicking against each other, the smell moving on fog: vapour, the brilliant lightning-tongue flashing, the eyes—beautiful, deadly, dogfishgreen eyes—staring, unblinking, emotionless, and the two heads coming closer and closer.

Peter wanted to pray and couldn't remember a prayer, he wanted to say something but couldn't remember a single word of English.

"Closer and closer." A voice in his head rang clearly. "Closer and closer until the stink of him makes you freeze."

The brilliant-hued right-end head raised, aimed at Peter's throat and began to move closer. The brilliant-hued left head followed suit and

all four eyes were staring at Peter.

He pressed against the tree, his eyes staring ahead, his lips moving in the chant the old man had taught him, lips moving, throat sealed as silent shut as that of He Who Would Sing

the right head poised itself to strike and suck his breath from him, the left head poised itself

then two dogfishgreen eyes met two other dogfishgreen
eyes
    left face saw right face
    the pulsing slowed
    the stenchfog eased to an occasional wisp
    the scales stopped clacking at each other
    Sisiutl shrank
    shrank
    back on himself
    two eyes staring into two eyes
    right face seeing left face
    who sees the other half of self sees Truth

THEY SAT AT THE KITCHEN TABLE ALL NIGHT, each locked in his own private struggle. The old man refused to go to bed, refused to even lie down on the sofa; he wheeled himself to his dance cape, wrapped it around his shoulders and wheeled himself back to the table, his face still carved from granite, his anger still flaring in his eyes. There was so much He Who Would Sing wanted to say, but he said nothing. He folded his hands in front of him and stared at them, stared at his fingers, almost cursing them for not being more fluent. The night wind howled at the chimney and He Who Would Sing thought of the Headless Woman, that insane hag with the cackling screech that shook the very foundations of courage. Under her scrawny arm she carried her head, the white hair streaming in the wind, and a basket of woven cedarbark into which she would pop the souls of the unwary. The only protection against her was the proper words, and when a person died the words had to be said so that the soul, on its way to the alternate reality, could not be captured by the Headless Woman. Tonight she was riding their chimney, and he put an extra load of wood into the stove to thwart her, for she hated smoke and heat, and one way to keep her out of your house was to keep the fire burning all the time.

The old man knew why He Who Would Sing was banking the stove: he, too, could hear the Headless Woman. He wondered if, at the time of his own death, the words inside the head of He Who Would Sing, the words that would never issue from the incomplete throat, would be protection for his soul on its journey. The women told him that they heard the Headless Woman often, but somehow the women seemed less frightened than the men, and when he asked why this was, the current Old Woman told him the legend of how Copper Woman had left her meat and her skin on the beach and using her bones as a broom had swept the sand of her mind clean and transmutated herself, becoming Old Woman. She waited for the time, the Time, and when it came, when a woman needed her, Old Woman would make herself known, and so every time a woman heard the wail of the Headless Woman, she would call in her heart and the Old Woman would answer and protect her, would come to her with that wisdom that has always allowed women to Endure, and the hags would be vanquished.

When dawn streaked the sky and the first rays of the sun came up out of the sea, the old man knew that the ear of creation was open and he sent his plea for protection. He hoped it was not too late.

THE DOOR OPENED and Peter stood outlined in the doorway. His face was scratched and dirty, tear-streaked and pale, but the hard lines around his young eyes were gone. His new jeans were torn at the knee and his new shirt was filthy, but his medicine-magic bag was still hanging around his neck. He tried to speak, but his throat only moved spasmodically.

He Who Would Sing rose, his hands started to move.

"Just you never mind," the old man muttered. "I already heard everything you got to say. I been listening to you all night. This here's between him'n'me.

Peter moved to the table and sat down, still trying to speak. He was crying again, his green eyes flooding, his lips working. He couldn't speak, but his small hand reached out slowly.

Peter's green eyes looking into the old man's raisin eyes

the old man's slanty raisin eyes staring into Peter's eyes and a wrinkled old brown hand reached out, took the small, grubby white hand, patted softly.

"It's okay, boy," the old man said softly in Nootka, "It's okay, you don't ever have to say 'sorry' to me. It's all going to be better than it was."

Peter rose quickly, moving around the table, sitting on the old man's lap, cuddling and sobbing, trying to tell about the Sisiutl, and the old man talked on in Nootka, calming the boy. Calming him with strange words in a foreign language. Calming him with touch. He Who Would Sing moved to hunker beside the two he loved. His powerful hands reached out, touching both his friends, adding his own messages, and the boy cried until he was asleep. He Who Would Sing moved Peter to the sofa and covered him with a blanket, then took the old man into his room, and finally the weary old Dreamspeaker allowed himself to take off his cape, lie down, and go to sleep.

HIS LEGS ACHED AND HIS CHEST HEAVED, sweat dribbled down his chest and turned the waistband of his jeans a darker blue, but still his feet shuffled and his throat throbbed with the steady four-beat chant of the initiate.

His medicine bag hung from his neck, bobbing softly against his chest with every movement; the white cotton sweatband around his forehead kept his eyes clear, fixed almost unblinkingly on the old man with the rattle, the silent man with the drum.

A dancer is a poet, a poet is magic, a dancer is a magic poet who knows the words told in the wind, a dancer is a magic poet whose wind words tell him the Truth, even the dreams he has are true, and the dancer poet is a priest who speaks only Truth, and so the initiated dancer-poet-priest is a Dreamspeaker.

One Dreamspeaker is Truth, two Dreamspeakers are Justice, three Dreamspeakers are Eternity and four Dreamspeakers are Rebirth. No evil can overcome the power of a Dreamspeaker, and if the initiation is painful, the rewards are great. There are those on the Island whose eyes see through the sea, whose ears hear past the wind, and some are men and some are women. There are those who can calm the angriest sea and soothe the most hurting soul, and some of these are men and some are women. There are those who Know without ever having to be told and some of these are men and some are women, and there are those who will Endure and some of these are men and some are women.

The rattle sounds continued, the soft drumming continued, and Peter danced on steadily.

For every wrong there are four rights. For every lie there are four truths. For every hurt there are four joys. For every death there are four lives.

There are four parts to a tree: roots, branches, trunk and leaves.

There are four winds.
There are four directions.
There are four seasons.
Four parts to life: being born, being young, being a parent and being dead. Death brings the fourth, the complete, the full; four makes it total, four makes it whole, and the final fourth is with us from birth.

The rattle ended, the drumming stopped; Peter stood, waiting, his sweat dripping to the floor. The Dreamspeaker sat in the wheeled chair and waited while the spirit dancer, the silent one, removed the dance capes and carefully folded them, replaced the rattle and drum, removed the ceremonial tokens and talismans. Only then did the old man speak, and only when the old man was again himself and not the Dreamspeaker, did Peter move.

"You done okay, boy. She's coming."

Peter nodded, relieved, and moved toward them, already tasting the coffee and sandwich he knew would soon be ready.

HAYSEEDS GET DOWN THE BACK OF YOUR NECK and bite as badly as any mosquito. Chaff catches in your nose and makes you sneeze, and it gets in your eyes and makes them tear, makes you blink and sometimes grab at your face unthinkingly. The sharp ends of the hay pierce your skin and cause an itch, and after half a day you wish you'd never even applied for the job. In the evening your muscles ache, your hands are raw, and you wonder how the mute manages to work so steadily, to lift the huge bales so easily, to work harder and longer than any of the other men. There seems to be no end to the work. There is work even for a young boy, especially if he has a good strong back, widening shoulders and a deep chest. Work behind the machine, in the dust, work with a large hanky over your mouth to keep you from choking in the dust.

At lunchtime you eat the meal the farmer's wife brings to the field in the back of a pickup, and you try not to blush when she says your muscles are growing bigger every day. She easily accepts the idea that He Who Would Sing is your uncle, and she laughs at the jokes you translate from fingertalk to words.

For ten days you work with the haying crew and when the work is finished and the farmer hands you your money, you know that the sunburn and chaff-itch were worth it all, the sore muscles and blistered palms were worth it, because he grins, winks, and says You be sure to come back next year, boy, you're going to be as good a worker as your uncle.

"Well, of course you are," the old man nodded, his voice faint. "Only stands to reason."

They went to bed early and slept soundly, and in the morning He Who Would Sing carried the old man to the small, shingled outhouse and waited until he was needed to carry the frail body back to the cabin. He put washwater in the enamel bowl and started breakfast, knowing the first clatter of the frying pan would waken the boy.

He laid strips of pork jowl in the frying pan, then turned, puzzled, toward the door. Three quick knocks and then the door opened sharply, and two RCMP stood outlined in the doorway. The old man seemed rooted, hands in mid-air, water dribbling back into the basin. Peter roused slowly, then caught sight of the RCMP. He leaped from the bed and dashed for the window.

Everything happened so swiftly there was no way to explain anything. The old man kept calling in Nootka No, don't, stop it, leave the boy alone, there's no need for this . . . Peter tried to avoid the heavy hands that reached for him, and He Who Would Sing forgot the lesson of the Raven and resorted to force. He fought desperately to pull the police away from the terrified child, and then the billyclub hit the side of his head and he slumped, half dazed, to the floor.

Peter screamed, kicked, fought, to no avail. Tucked securely under a uniformed arm, he was carried to the police car and deposited in the back seat.

A heavy wire grill between back seat and front, no door handles on the inside of the door—the back seat of a police car is one of the most secure jail cells in Canada.

7

THEY DIDN'T TAKE HIM DIRECTLY TO THE FACILITY. They took him first to a juvenile detention wing of the main holding facility in the city. He looked around the small room, a cell really, looking at the many many names scratched on the walls, the insulting graffiti left behind by untold numbers of boys.

"I don't want to be here," he said quietly. "I want to go home and be with my grandpa and my uncle." Nobody seemed to pay attention to him, they just looked through him and closed the door. When he tried to open it, the knob wouldn't turn and the door was locked.

In the morning Anna came to see him. She smiled at him, and for the first time in a long time, for the first time since he was little, he could smile back at her. He even made the first move, and cuddled her.

"I was worried sick, Peter," she half laughed, half cried, holding him close.

"I don't want to stay here. Please, Anna, tell them to let me go back to Grandpa and He Who Would Sing."

"Tell me about it, Peter," she said, but he knew by the way her smile died and her eyes darkened that she wasn't sure she could get him back where he belonged.

"We've got a little old house," he said, letting his body help him tell the story, feeling the lessons in storytelling having their effect. "There's only one door to the house, but there are four windows, and Grandpa and He Who Would Sing have a bedroom with two small beds, but I sleep on the sofa in the big room."

He told her about the wood carvings and the big black stove, he told her about picking berries and making jam, about growing the corn they ate slathered in butter and about peeling the skins off the tomatoes.

THE COURTROOM WASN'T A REGULAR COURTROOM, not like the ones on television. Family court and juvenile court both got held in what looked like just a big room, with a big table surrounded by chairs. A picture of the Queen looked down on them. She looked like a nice lady, her hands neatly folded across the front of her nice white dress with the blue ribbon across the chest, her eyes staring across the room to the other wall.

A side door opened and Grandpa was wheeled in by He Who Would Sing. They were both freshly shaven, with new haircuts, and they were both wearing new pants and shirts. Grandpa had a tie fastened at his throat and He Who Would Sing winked and with his hands made comment on their city-feller appearance. Peter ran to them, not caring that everyone could see him crying, and he sat on the old man's knee and cuddled closely. The old man murmured in Nootka and He Who Would Sing made rapid hand flashings and all Peter could say was "I knew you'd come, I just knew you'd come." Anna came over. He knew it was her job to keep an eye on him, but he also knew she came because she wanted to help him. "This is Anna. She's my worker."

"We're proud to meet a friend of Peter's," Grandpa said

quietly, offering her his hand. "This is my son He Who Would Sing," and the mute offered his huge hand.

"I'm so glad Peter met you," and then she wanted to say more, but her throat wouldn't work.

"Well, so are we," Grandpa agreed, and then they just smiled at each other and he patted her hand again.

Peter saw John and some of the others from the facility, and when John looked hard at him, Peter thought he almost knew all the things John was trying to say with his eyes. He wanted to answer the Why, he wanted to say You didn't do anything wrong it was just . . . but he knew that John couldn't read his face, couldn't read the answers Peter was sending with his eyes.

"It's okay, boy, you'll get your chance," Grandpa whispered, and Anna nodded, her quick smile flickering reassuringly.

A man from the welfare office got up and told how the silent one and the old man had suddenly appeared at his desk demanding to talk to someone about adopting a boy. He explained that it had been very difficult to even fill in the form required.

"Mr. Seward,"—Peter realized that was Grandpa's real name—doesn't seem to know how old he is, and Mr. Thomas,"—Peter supposed that was He Who Would Sing—"cannot speak at all and so we had to communicate with written notes." He told about going out to the cabin, "a small unpainted frame dwelling," and about the unfinished sink, the missing pipe, the well with the old bucket and the new rope. He told about the shingled outhouse at the end of the path, and about the lack of washing machine, electricity, or a separate bedroom for Peter. Peter wanted to tell about the birds' nest in the eaves, the trees for climbing and the rocks for jumping from, but he knew he would have to wait for his chance.

The psychiatrist from the facility got up and talked a bit but Peter didn't understand what he was saying. Then the doctor told the results of all the tests they had taken. John told about the fight in the dining room and the bedwetting, about the seizure and Peter's sudden disappearance from the infirmary. Then it was Anna's turn. She told about things Peter had totally forgotten, about the sores on his backside and the bugs in his hair. She told about things Peter could remember, like having to pack his things in a shopping bag because the mother was sick, and about having to move once because he'd been bad, and about the time he'd had to move without anybody being able to tell him why.

"We've been totally unable to find an answer for Peter's problems," she said softly, smiling at him, "and I feel that possibly Peter has found an answer for himself."

"Are you suggesting the boy should be placed with Mr. Seward and Mr. Thomas?" the judge asked, his old blue eyes looking into hers.

"If it was up to me," she replied with a small laugh, "I would have no hesitation. Unfortunately, because of Peter's conviction and his placement at the facility, it isn't up to me any more; I can only strongly recommend that we start looking at things from Peter's point of view; he's never gone this long in his life without an explosion of some kind."

They asked questions of Grandpa and He Who Would Sing, who answered with his fingers and was interpreted by both the old man and the young boy.

"He says," Peter chose his words carefully, "that he hasn't worked at a steady job before because he never needed much money. He says if you want, he'll get a job and work all the time."

"What he means," the old man added gently, "is we never had any need for electric things and money, but if it's the only way you'll let us keep our boy, we'll get them."

Then the judge stared down at everyone for a while, and he checked some notes he had made. "No society," he said slowly, "can call itself civilized unless in its dealings with people it has both mercy and compassion. As a society we must at all times try to work toward a better life for those most helpless of our citizens. As has already been pointed out in testimony, we were unable to find any answer for Peter, and so he was forced to take matters into his own hands. I recommend that both Mr. Seward and Mr. Thomas be given the same rights and considerations as would be granted to natural parents in such a case." Peter felt the stiffness going out of his shoulders, he heard the sigh He Who Would Sing heaved. "I further recommend that they be given full assistance in regard to transportation and accommodation so that they may be included as fully as possible in all future treatment for Peter. They will be given every opportunity to visit Peter at the facility and it is to be hoped that treatment will be so structured as to in future include such things as overnight and weekend visits ..."

Peter was the first one to realize what it was the judge was saying. He heard the word "facility" and felt the shutters coming down over his eyes, felt the mask slipping back over his face, and then he was standing, mouth open, one long horrible scream coming from his throat, a scream that cut into the old man as surely as a knife cuts into the belly of a fish, a scream that turned the knuckles of the mute's hands white, a scream that struck Anna like a physical blow, and he was still screaming when they carried him from the room, carried him past the picture of the lady in the white dress with the blue ribbon.

AND THEN HE WAS SITTING IN THE OFFICE, sunk deep into a big padded chair, and across the desk from him the psychiatrist with the hooded eyes was sitting, staring at him, his mouth moving, and so Peter forced his ears open.

"I'm going to show you some cards, Peter," the words said, "and I want you to look at them carefully, and tell me what you think of when you look at them; tell me what they make you think of."

He held up a card and Peter stared at the shape; it looked like a bat, or like a flying fox, or like . . . he forced himself to study it carefully, and he felt his face changing itself, making itself look like the face of someone who was very carefully considering.

"It looks like . . . shit," he said softly.

The psychiatrist didn't blink, he just held up another.

"It looks like shit," Peter said, satisfied.

Another card.

"It looks like shit." He was quite certain now.

And another. "Shit."

Finally the psychiatrist put his hands on top of the cards and stared at Peter, and Peter knew the psychiatrist knew that they would all look like shit. Forever they would look like shit. All of them. Forever.

AND SO THEY LED HIM BACK TO HIS ROOM and took his clothes away from him, giving him a pair of facility pyjamas to wear. He crossed to his bed and sat on it, wondering if anybody had yet noticed there was no goal for the hockey players to shoot at, no way to score and win the game.

"Peter." John spoke from the door. Peter made his head turn, and saw John standing holding some pills and a glass of water. "You might as well take them, Peter, they'll only give you a needle if you don't."

Peter took the pills, put them in his mouth, washed them down with the water and then opened his mouth to prove to John that he had swallowed the pills.

"That's a boy." John tried to smile.

Peter dropped the glass on the floor. The water spread in a puddle. His eyes locked with John's, Peter stood up slowly. Very deliberately he opened the front of his pyjamas and began to urinate, spraying the floor, the wall, the chair, the bed. Then he ripped the front of his pyjama top open, the buttons popping, falling to the floor to roll past the unbreakable drinking glass. He reached for his pillow and threw it into the puddle of spilled water and urine.

John backed slowly for the door, staring at Peter, staring straight into a rage and a madness he had never before seen.

THE CORRIDOR STRETCHED LONG, LONG, LONG, and down it moved a file of grey-clad youngsters, walking in loose order, not marching, but moving two by two, neatly, down the hallway to the lunchroom. Peter moved with them, feeling the pills from last night working with the pills from this morning, feeling his arms heavy and his eyes dull. He hadn't wakened in time for breakfast and they had let him sleep in the jumble of torn sheets and overturned furniture, hoping when he wakened the rage would be sufficiently diluted by pills to be manageable.

He stood in line quietly, his tray in his hands, moving routinely along the food line. When he had his lunch, he moved to the place that had been his before he ran away, and he sat down on the bench, staring at his food. The other boys had heard him cursing and throwing furniture until late into the night, and they all eyed him carefully, remembering that this was the kid who wouldn't take anything from anyone. Peter carefully lined up his knife, fork and spoon, moved his milk glass to the safe position, and when everything on his tray was Just So

he picked up his bowl of soup and calmly threw it against the wall. Followed by his bread and butter. Then his glass of milk.

The staff moved toward him quickly, and were sprayed from every side by flying chicken pot pie as all the boys took their cue from Peter and joined in. Vegetables ran down the wall; the heavyset man from the kitchen staff slipped in the white sauce and nearly fell, and then the chairs were flying, the bigger boys were sending the steam table crashing to the floor, and the little boys were racing out of the dining room, heading for the bathrooms.

Peter moved calmly through the growing riot, heading for the schoolroom. He walked in and went from desk to desk, methodically overturning furniture, dumping books on the floor, spilling ink, scattering pencils, crayons and paints, and finally throwing things from the teacher's desk through the windows.

The bathroom sinks were plugged and overflowing, the water falling in small cascades to the floor, joining the water that was gushing from the toilets, effectively plugged with mops and entire rolls of toilet paper. The mirrors were all smashed, the floor littered with broken glass and soggy toilet paper, and smeared across the empty mirror frames were the words SHIT SHIT SHIT. A small boy with blond hair and blue eyes scooped more of it from the plugged toilet and flung it against the wall, laughing happily at the *plop*, and then reached into the toilet tank to twist and pull out the flush mechanism. Peter watched him leave the bathroom and run down the hallway into a bedroom, to appear a moment later dragging a burning blanket behind him, running from room to room spreading fire, smoke and happy laughter.

The swimming pool was littered with chairs, lockers, towels, benches, floating and half-floating debris, and the big boys were using the fire axes to smash open the lockers and shatter the tile floor. All the overhead sprinklers were responding to the smoke from burning paper. Floors were awash, bedding ruined, the audio visual training room was a total wreck and the pool tables in the recreation rooms were demolished.

Peter felt the pills and the fatigue of his extended rampage pulling at him, and he walked to a quiet corner of the reading room and sat on the floor ripping pages from books and trying hard not to fall asleep.

John and two other counsellors came into the room and moved toward Peter; he saw the gleam of a needle, felt a quick prick in his arm and it was with a feeling of near relief that he let himself fall into the soft black sea that sped coolly from his inner elbow, up his arm, turned the corner at his shoulder and then

the overhead light spun rapidly

the floor fell from beneath him

and John caught him as he slumped sideways, eyes rolled back, mouth still half open

HE WHO WOULD SING REACHED FOR THE RAVEN RATTLE and shook it softly. He had known when the police left with Peter that there weren't enough words in anybody's throat, anybody's hands, or anybody's mind to keep the ravens of death away from the cabin. He had seen the first raven settle on the cedar tree before he could even get himself up off the floor and move to the bitterly sobbing old man. By the time he had wiped the blood from his face and put a cold cloth on the growing lump on his head there had been three ravens perched on the branch of the giant cedar. And now there were four.

He had taken the old man into town, taken him to the welfare office, done everything he could do to try to get the boy back, even managing to pretend to the old man that he had faith, that he believed the sunshine would come back and the cold wind stop blowing. But when the judge had said what he had said and Peter had screamed that knife-scream, the old man had shrunk in on himself, his hands becoming suddenly two trembling leaves on an alder tree, his eyes staring past this world to something different.

"I don't want dirt in my nose, son," the old man managed weakly. "I want the wind in my hair and the smell of the sea."

He Who Would Sing could only nod, tears streaming from his eyes.

"In the old days, when this land was ours, we didn't stuff our dead into a hole in the ground. We carved a mortuary pole and put the dead inside, or else built a platform high in a tree where they could be part of the wind, the rain, the grass, and the night."

He Who Would Sing nodded again, his lips moving in the words of the dirge, his eyes watching the last breath coming from the withered lips.

"It's not the end, son. We don't ever end, you and me. Four makes her complete. Being a child, being a parent, being old and being dead. Not finished, son. Just complete." Then the pale lips tried to smile, the gnarled hand tried to reach out . . .

THE STLALACUM LIGHTS WERE DANCING SLOWLY, their tinkling call muted and strange. Peter opened his eyes, looked around slowly. He was in a different room, not his own room at all. There was no big black stove, no kitchen table, no wooden statues and carvings. Just a high, narrow institutional bed and a window with a heavy wire mesh between him and the glass. And yet he could hear the sound of the cedar rattle, a soft, slow rhythm filling his ears.

He looked at the wall and thought as hard as he could, sending his third eye through the wall, reaching for the cedar rattle, reaching.

He could see the sun coming up out of the bed of the sea, could see the arbutus trees reaching toward the sky, their bark slowly peeling, falling, reforming endlessly. Past the arbutus trees the white spiralling Sisiutl trees pointed to the clouds, standing guard on the point. There were birds singing and small animals were coming awake, the ear of creation was open and

high in a cedar tree He Who Would Sing was lashing something to a platform. Peter recognized the carving tools, the bead loom, he could see jars of jam and preserves, some money and

Grandfather, sleeping peacefully, his hair blowing in the wind, his nostrils filled with the smell of the sea, his ears hearing the song of the birds, his face

stiff and not warming with the rising sun

and the sound of the cedar rattle grew

grew and merged with Peter's sobs. He climbed out of bed

123

and moved to the door, but it was locked. He tried to shake the door open, tried to pull the door from its frame

and then Raven was cawing never use force, and the Copper Woman-Old Woman was telling him about Time; the Stlalacum were asking him if he knew the difference between transmutation and transmigration, and he thought of the difference between becoming something and going somewhere . . .

JOHN WALKED DOWN THE HALLWAY, turned to open Peter's door. The bed stood in the middle of the room, pulled away from its place by the wall, the blankets on the floor, the blue and white striped mattress cover staring accusingly

back at the distended green eyes that stared, frozen, from the blue-tinged swollen face.

"Oh my God," John gasped, wishing he could tear his eyes away from the blue-tipped fingers and toes, the protruding purplish tongue, the lips congested to a near black. Lines dug into his face like the lines in the face of an incredibly ancient man, pain etched still in his eyes, his hair hanging limp, his neck twisted awkwardly, Peter's body hung from the knotted strips of sheet fastened to the overhead light fixture.

THE MUTE STOOD IN THE SMALL CABIN, looking around at what was left. The beaded belt, the old ball glove, a pile of comic books, a half-finished carving of the Snipe dancing, and he reached out to touch the medicine bag that had been ripped from Peter's neck in the struggle with the police. He gathered the treasures and put them in a small woven cedar basket and took them with him.

He sat on the platform beside the earthly remains of his

adopted father. Inside his mind he said the words that needed saying, the words that would keep the Headless Woman
from interfering with the journey he had to make. To change
form is often painful. To travel from one reality to the other
is always lonely. To shed a form because of cowardice, fear, or
shame is a sin, but to knowingly change form and shape, to
knowingly choose to travel from one plane of reality to another is the choice all the children of the free ones have. Old
Woman made her choice and left her bag of meat and skin on
the beach.

He Who Would Sing made his choice. His powerful legs
straightened, his feet pressed against the wooden peg placed
against both triggers

a double load of SSG tore through his mouth

What was left of his body slumped against the bonds with
which he had fastened himself to the bole of the cedar tree;
the last damp shards of what had been his voiceless head splat-
tered wetly to the earth, giving back to her that which she had
given to him

and the ravens flew, cawing, from the small clearing

flying across the sky
flying

and where the clear water stream bubbled over the granite
rocks a young boy jerked around, pointing, pointing to where
a flock of ravens swooped low, then headed away
    except

for the one who fell to earth, fell willingly, delivering a soul, tumbling into the waist-high yellow grass.

THE OLD MAN MOVED SWIFTLY ON STRONG LEGS, racing with the boy toward the hilltop. Peter reached out and took his grandfather's hand, his laughter rising on the wind.

"Listen to him, Grandpa, listen to him holler!"

"I told you, boy," Grandpa laughed, "I told you that was one hell of a sound!"

And He Who Would Sing, did. Letting it all pour from his throat, a rich song that blended with the laughter of a healthy young boy and a loving old man. Death, the fourth, the constant companion who made it complete, smiled and rose from the yellow grass, rose back to the heavens on the wings of the raven, a black bird who used to be a white bird who used to be a god-person, a black bird whose voice is a sharp stone to cut the day.

And He Who Would Sing was singing for the matriarch and her women, singing for the ears of creation, for the men who would one day be Dreamspeakers and the men who had been Dreamspeakers, singing for the women who had been Dreamspeakers and the women who would be Dreamspeakers, singing to the ear of creation, singing with the voice he had always known was his. Singing to celebrate something he had heard for the first time after death, the sound of a healthy child, laughing happily.

The Fiction of Anne Cameron

"Anne Cameron's fictional voice is unique in Canada. She can cuss like a logger or set down words as tender as lullabies. Her West Coast, small-town characters, like her prose, are rough and tough, sweet 'n' tender."

—*Ottawa Citizen*

"The anger and passion with which Cameron writes lift the ordinary into something stronger."

—*Quill & Quire*

"Cameron understands the way a woman's work affects every other sphere of her life."

—*Feminist Bookstore News*

Dahlia Cassidy

Novel • 6 x 9 • 264 pages, paperback • 1-55017-344-8

Daughters of Copper Woman

Legends • 5¼ x 7½ • 200 pages, paperback • 1-55017-245-X

Hardscratch Row

Novel • 6 x 9 • 378 pages, paperback • 1-55017-290-5

Sarah's Children

Novel • 5½ x 8½ • 288 pages, paperback • 1-55017-274-3

Those Lancasters

Novel • 6 x 9 • 398 pages, paperback • 1-55017-227-1

Aftermath

Novel • 6 x 9 • 400 pages, paperback • 1-55017-193-3

Selkie

Novel • 6 x 9 • 192 pages, paperback • 1-55017-152-6

The Whole Fam Damily

Novel • 6 x 9 • 264 pages, paperback • 1-55017-134-8

DeeJay & Betty

Novel • 6 x 9 • 264 pages, paperback • 1-55017-112-7

Kick the Can

Novel • 6 x 9 • 160 pages, paperback • 1-55017-039-2

Escape to Beulah

Novel • 6 x 9 • 236 pages, paperback • 1-55017-029-5

South of an Unnamed Creek

Novel • 6 x 9 • 200 pages, hardcover • 1-55017-013-9

Women, Kids & Huckleberry Wine

Short stories • 6 x 9 • 258 pages, paperback • 0-920080-68-5

AVAILABLE AT BETTER BOOKSTORES OR

HARBOUR PUBLISHING

P.O. Box 219

Madeira Park, BC, Canada V0N 2H0

Phone (604) 883-2730
Fax (604) 883-9451
Toll-free order line 1 800 667-2988
Toll-free fax order line 1 877 604-9449
Email orders@harbourpublishing.com
Website www.harbourpublishing.com